WAITING PERIOD

Also by Hubert Selby Jr.

Last Exit to Brooklyn

The Demon

The Room

Requiem for a Dream

Song of the Silent Snow

The Willow Tree

WAITING PERIOD

Hubert Selby Jr.

MARION BOYARS
NEW YORK • LONDON

First published in the United States and Great Britain in 2002 by
MARION BOYARS PUBLISHERS LTD
237 E 39th Street, New York NY 10016
24 Lacy Road, London SW15 1NL

www.marionboyars.co.uk

Distributed in Australia and New Zealand by Peribo Pty Ltd,
58 Beaumont Road, Kuring-gai, NSW 2080

10 9 8 7 6 5 4 3 2 1

A CIP catalog record for this book is available from the Library of Congress
A CIP catalogue record for this book is available from the British Library

ISBN 0-7145-3071-9 Hardcover

Printed and bound in Great Britain by the Bath Press, CPI Group.

Set in Bembo 12/16 pt

This book is dedicated to
THE INQUISITION

'Everything has a purpose on this earth, and all things fulfill their purpose – seaweed, dung beetles, parasites – without agonizing or questioning. We are the only part of Creation that is blinded by desires and thus ignore our particular purpose, individually and collectively, and spend our lives in mad pursuit of nothingness'

Gottfried Llewelyn-Jones
Anatomy and Evolution of Universal Madness

…but obviously the best way is with sleeping pills and a plastic bag over your head…sitting in a tub filled with water, I think. Sounds easy enough. Sort of peaceful. Go to sleep and thats it. Yeah, I guess…if you dont get sick and throw up all the damn pills… Yeah, lying in a bathtub covered in my own puke, so woozy I cant get out—wait, how would I be covered with puke, I have a plastic bag over my head…o krist, I/d be suffocated by my own vomit, ugh, thats disgusting and I might be too weak to rip a hole in the bag or get it off and I just sit there aware of whats happening, spinning, falling…falling into what? Who knows. Whatever you fall into…some abyss I guess…down, down…down into hell…or at least purgatory, at least thats what the catholics say. Even the ones that dont have purgatory have a hell. Well…what the hell…

But suppose I suddenly change my mind and call 911? What happens then? I/d end up in a funny farm with millions of people asking me questions, driving me nuts wanting to know why I did it, as if living in this world is so wonderful you must be crazy to want to leave it. They knock themselves out trying to live longer and longer, just another year, thats all… Yeah, live to be 70 or 80 or 90 or krist knows how long. For what? And who the hell are they to say Im nuts because Ive had enough of this lousy world? The hell withem. Bugging me with their questions: why did you do this? why did you do that? why dont you like this? why dont you like that? why dont you exercise more? join a gym? yeah, thats it, get in shape, drink Evian water, learn to dance, go to clubs, meet some chicks, join a church and meet some chicks, mingle more, socialize, expand your circle of friends, have a drink or two, dont be so stiff, start smoking marijuana, chill, meet some chicks

and

suppose the lazy bastards dont get me to the hospital in time? Yeah, they fuck around and I dont get my stomach pumped in time and I become paralyzed, strapped down in a bed with diapers on, staring up at the ceiling, thinking…thats all, just thinking, thinking…unable to move, totally dependent on people to take care of me and you know what kind of job they do, let you lie in your dirty diapers for days, smelling like death, totally humiliated, back ripped open with bed sores and you cant say anything, not even moan or cry…just think, think, 24 hours a day, thinking…jesus, a five minute ride to the hospital and it takes them more than half an hour, fucking assholes. Ive heard of that happening. More than once… Many, many times. Like that woman in Jersey. It was years before they pulled the plug. Young too. I wonder if she was trying to check out or just overdosed? I dont know. Anyway, its chancy. Who knows what happens when you get all those pills in you? You might call anyone. Its not safe.

But the old Roman way is so messy. I guess it really works, but my god… Sitting in a tub of hot water and slashing your wrists and ankles… I dont know. I guess you need a really sharp razor blade, or one of those razor knifes. How would you hold on to it after the first slice? Everything all bloody and slippery. You could drop the knife and by then the waters all bloody and you cant see the damn knife and you have to feel around for it and probably cut your hand all up and maybe pass out before you have a chance to finish the job and someone finds you and gets you to the hospital and they sew you up and here come all those people again wanting to know whats wrong then all the questions and the next thing you know youre in the funny farm…shit! End up in the same place. Just cant win. Even if you dont drop the knife how can you rip one arm open from wrist to elbow, then use that arm to open up the other arm? Youd have to be fast as hell. Have to be sure to do the ankles first. Yeah. Thats important. Ankles first. Jesus, that must really hurt. Like the time I tripped over that piece of barbed wire and slashed my ankle. God, that was painful. Topped off with tetanus shots… And you have to do both of them. Damn, I dont know which way you cut them, up…or across. I/d have to close my eyes. Krist, if you do it right youd be able to see right down to the bone, all those muscles and tendons and everything god what a repulsive…ugh. How in the hell did they do it? Or Hari Kari? Thats really crazy. In…all the way in, and up and over… No, impossible. You have to be born into that. Its just not for occidentals. More than cultural, obviously religious. Its beyond me…or maybe just fall on your sword…yeah, thats a good one… First you need a damn sword, then you have to practice for years to find out how to do it, who comes up with those crazy ideas? Knights in shining armor. Idiots. Why not, the world is filled with idiots. One benefit of modern warfare, you dont have to fall on your sword if you make a mistake. Dont have to carry one of those damn things either…unless youre English. They probably still have them. Think West Point Cadets do too…who knows, maybe they all do, makes them feel like big brave men to go clanking around with their swords…yeah, wonder if the women have to wear one too? Might make them feel too manly, krist, whats going on? Seems like the madness of the world is poisoning my mind. Why not just jump out a window???? How in the hell does it get so complicated? Why cant you just kill yourself? Who needs all these rituals? Something simple, like a bullet in the brain. Quick. Neat. Goodbye. Thats all there is there aint no more. Tellem Porky: Th Th Th Thats all Folks…

Actually thats a good idea. A gun. Never liked them, dont know anything about them. People always shooting each other. Ignorant goofs. First class knuckleheads. Shoot their own kids in the dark. Sick American macho madness. Maybe they should go back to swords. Might save a lot of innocent lives. But even guns dont work sometimes. They say you have to put the barrel in your mouth—must taste disgusting. Been people just grazed their temple, or shot themselves in the chest and missed their heart. Gotta put the barrel in your mouth...and point it up I suppose. The kind with a long, skinny barrel. Pistol I guess. Cant be too small or I may just crack my teeth. Something big. 38? Magnum? Theyre bigger and have barrels...I think. How do you get one? Yeah, sure, in a gun store, but how do you actually buy one? Hey mister, let me have a gun with a barrel thatll reach the back of my mouth, something in spearmint or cinnamon flavor. Shit. Probably have to fill out a dozen forms now and wait. Five days I think. Krist, there they go again. Cant do anything without them looking over your shoulder. What the hell business is it of theirs what you do with your life? You work your butt off, give them half your money—give? they take it and if you try to do anything about it they throw you in jail for that too. How in the hell can it be illegal to take your own life? What horseshit. What pure, unadulterated horseshit. A felony! Can you believe it, a felony to kill yourself...or at least to attempt it and fail. And if you do fail they lock you up. Can you believe that? They lock you up. Wonder what they do if you succeed? Take your corpse to court before they bury you?

Is it true that you killed yourself dead?

'...'

The accused is ordered to answer the courts question.

'. . .'

If you continue to refuse to answer you will be declared in contempt of this court.

'. . .'

Very well then, you will be remanded to the county jail and held in custody until you indicate to the court that you are ready to answer the court/s questions. Can you believe that? A felony to take your own life. The only thing you have that is truly your own and they tell you what you can and can not do with it. You have to live whether you like it or not. The church tyrants say you do not have the right to take your own life because you did not create you so only god can take what he has given. Suicide is an unforgivable sin. They not only want to control you while youre living, they want to haunt you in your grave! Aint that some ridiculous horseshit. These 'holy men of god' kill millions and millions of people in the name of god, but you cant take your own life, your own pathetic life. God gave me life. Shit! Maybe god can make a tree, but it doesnt have any thing to do with me. And anyway, where do they get off making that religious bullshit a law. Well, it makes sense, the government wants all the consumers it can get. I can understand why people want to blow up the government. All those sleazy little slime-balls. Krist, they irritate the hell out of me. Shootings too good for those leeches. You need to strangle the blood suckers. Can you believe it, charging a dead man with a felony! I wonder how much a gun costs? Even if you wanted to shoot those bastards you have to be a consumer. They got you coming and going.

Put it on your charge card and those ghouls will take the fillings out of your teeth to get their money. I wonder how much gold I have in my mouth? Maybe I should find an old Nazi, theyd be able to tell at a glance how much my mouth is worth. Dont imagine there are any hiding out here. Guess not too many left by now. Krist, those vermin did all right. The most hideous bunch of bureaucrats the world has ever seen, and they live for ever…healthy, happy, and money up the kazoo. How in the hell does that work? How can they do the things they do and never miss a minutes sleep, never feel guilty? Guess its no different than murdering 'nigras' in the south, or the Pat Robertson gang wanting to 'eliminate' the gay and 'feminist' communities. Krist, what a holocaust we would have if those 'men of god' ever got in power. The Inquisition would look like the proverbial childrens picnic. Wonder how many brownie points I/d get for each one of those I sent to the man in the white night gown before I check out? If I were giving them out I/d get a whole bus load of them. I thought I was kidding, but thats not such a bad idea. I could really go happily into that good night if I could check a few of those festering pus pockets out first. Ah…whats the point of even thinking about it, I cant do it. Better just stick with blowing my head off. Thats the only thing that makes sense. Just no way out of this godawful mess. Cant get through this blackness. Its got fangs and claws and constantly chews my flesh and rips the eyes out of my sockets jesus krist Im just chewed and chewed and chewed but never killed…never. Only perpetual dying.

Thats the thing about torture, first theres the threat of death, then theres the promise of death, but you are never blessed with the simple gift of death. Oh, whats the use of all this madness of mind and body? I cant move. Cant get out of this apartment. How long? Days? Weeks? But I do get out sometimes. Sooner or later I will get up and open that door and leave this building and get a gun. Sooner or later the demons will sleep, if only for a moment. They always do. I/ll be ready. Oh yes, this time I shall be ready, as well as willing and able. I know just where the shop is. And the hours. I/ll get there. Sooner or later. Its inevitable.

Hi, what can I do for you?

Well…I was thinking of buying a gun.

Yeah, well thats something we have plenty of. Funny how thats true of gun shops, eh? So, what did you have in mind, AK-47, pellet pistol, elephant gun, bazooka, bubble gum that is, what can I do you for?

Well, Im not sure, you know. I mean—

You thinking in terms of a rifle, a handgun, a—

Oh yeah. A handgun. Nothing big, you know. A handgun.

Well, come over here. Got a whole display case of handguns. Target pistols, semiautomatics, revolvers, 22s, 38s, 357s, 45s.

Damn, sure are a lot of them, arent there?

Yeah, something for every need. I assume youre not a hit man, right?

Huh? What—

Relax. Only kidding. I mean you really dont know from guns, right?

Yeah.

Well, depends on what you want it for. Protection, right? Something to have around the house in case the moving men from B&E show up at 3 in the morning, right?

Huh, I dont—

Intruders. Burglars. 2nd storey men. Sneak thieves.

Oh…yes, yes. Protection. Cant be too careful these days, uh can you?

Thats right buddy. I got one of each of these at home.

Huh?

Joshing man. Just putting you on. A little joke.

Oh. Yeah.

So, what do you think youd like? Personally, I think you should go for this 357 here. Good weight. Good accuracy. Plenty of stopping power. Hit a guy anywhere and hes not moving. Bet your ass on that. Here give it a heft.

Oh, I dont—

Hey, its not loaded. Comeon, Im crazy not stupid. Relax. Here. Just see how it feels in your hand. Yeah, thats it.

Oh, its heavy. I had no idea handguns were so heavy.

Yeah, they look light in the movies, dont they? The way they run around firing at everything that moves.

Yeah…

Youll get used to the weight. I assume youre going to

take it to a range and get used to firing it—

Oh yes—

Which reminds me, youll need a cleaning kit. Important you keep your weapon cleaned and oiled. Dont want it blowing up in your face.

Oh my god, no. Absolutely not. Oh no, no.

Dont worry about anything you buy here. All guaranteed. No weapon you purchase from me will ever misfire due to a defect in the weapon. Guaranteed. Go ahead, check it out. Imagine having someone shove that in your face. Youd shit a brick, right?

The more I look at it the bigger it gets.

Go ahead, hold it out in front of you and pull the trigger a few times.

It doesnt work, I cant pull it back.

You got the safety on.

Safety?

Yeah. Haha, you really are a novice. Look, see this, its the safety, so it cant accidentally be discharged. Have to push it over like this.

Oh, I see. But does a set of instructions come with it, I mean how will I know what to do??

I/ll be sure to give you some diagrams and a pamphlet. With the cleaning kit. But make sure you go to the range like I said.

Oh yes. Definitely. Dont want any mishaps.

Right. So, I assume youll want a box of ammo with that.

I guess so, if you think I should.

No good without it, right?

Not much.

Okay, let me fill in this form so we can get you approved. Put this information into the computer and we/ll get the ok before I finish wrapping this up. Great system now, no more waiting period. Check you out just like that. Unless youre an excon or escaped murderer or something.

No, no problem with—

Damn, now what in the hell does that mean?

Something wrong?

With the system. Cant process the request. Let me give them a call…

Well, whats wrong? What did they say?

Theres some sort of glitch in the software. Its new and I guess they havent ironed out all the wrinkles. Afraid youre going to have to wait a few days until they straighten out the problem.

A few days?

I/ll give you a call. This number, right?

What???? Oh yeah, thats my number. But theres nothing I can do? Go to the police station?

Wont do you any good. Its all the same system and the computer aint working.

Oh…

Hey, its alright. Dont look so glum. I/ll have this all ready for you as soon as the ok comes in an all youll have to do is come an pick it up. Hey, its alright buddy. Comeon, perk up. You look like you just lost your best friend or something. Its just a couple of days. Hey, if you get robbed before I get the ok, I/ll give you the gun for nothing, gratis. Hows that?

I just thought…

So now I just sit here and wait. The rotten system isnt functioning. Always the system. Cant escape it. This stinking lousy life. Just wants to torture me. I finally find a purpose to my life and they thwart me. Wont even let me kill myself for krists sake. What kind of madness is that? They just keep squeezing until theres nothing left. The torturous world just gets smaller and smaller until youre locked in a fucking closet, sealed in the son of a bitch. A living horror story. Buried alive. Hearing every grain of dirt falling on your coffin, thumping through your ears, your head and down through your body to your toes and back again, thump, thump…and scratch…scratch the wood, a dead tree, trying to get out jesus krist, how can they do that to you? Can you imagine what it must sound like to be nailed in a casket with a ton of dirt on top of you and youre scratching the wood? It must feel like ice picks going into your ears and eyes, long thin picks of pure ice o krist, how long will it take them to give me an ok? Assholes and their corrupt systems. Theyre never bothered by their mistakes. We/re the ones who always have to pay. No matter what they do they get away with it and we have to pick up the pieces and pay their bills. They make your life unbearable and then they mangle their system so you cant even kill yourself. The Inquisition never dies. I finally get to that point where I have a purpose, a plan, I know I can stick a gun in my mouth and pull the trigger, and get a gun and they pull this shit. DAMN. DAMN!!!! First they make it impossible to live, then impossible to die. Wait. Yeah, sure, just wait. Sit and let the air force itself into your lungs. If only I could just stop breathing, but no, that would be too easy. Those rotten bastards! Theyre the ones who should die. Theyre the ones I should use the gun on. Maybe one of those automatic ones. Mow them down just like in the movies. Yeah…thered be no way they could connect the killings to me. I dont know them and they dont know me. No connection. No notes, no warnings, and certainly no letters to the press. No declaration of purpose and intent. Just apparently random killings. I really understand those post office employees who go berserk and start shooting co-workers. But thats stupid. The result of being crazed with rage. No, thats not the way to go about it. Calm and quiet. First select the ones who are responsible for this mess, well, yeah, thats dumb. There are millions of them. Most of them you cant get to. You just cant go too far up the ladder. Have to accept that simple fact. But there are plenty who perpetuate the oppression and who are accessible. There are thousands of them. No pattern. Always random. Different organizations, different agencies. Different parts of the country. One from column A and one from column B. Obviously cant use the same gun. Except maybe for a few in one area…like out on the coast. Let them concentrate on one obvious area while I/ll cover the rest of the country, using different means of eliminating the vermin. Best to start with the VA and

HMOs. Just shoot a couple of those bastards. Nothing fancy. Just blow their rotten heads off. Bam! Just 3 or 4. Well...maybe half a dozen, or so. Theyll know one person killed them all and never tie them in with an occasional bank president or CEO or redneck cop. Can use several guns. And knives. Fire. Garottes. Explosives. They say you can learn how to make bombs on the Internet. And poisons. Biological weapons. Contaminate a needle and stick someone in a crowd. Or a blow-gun type thing. Like the old dart guns. Strong spring in a cigarette holder. Walk by and hit them in the neck. Theyd probably brush that area as if they were bitten by a bug and knock the little dart away and there would be no evidence of the sting. They would simply suddenly have a deadly virus and die of natural causes. Not too many. Nothing obvious. E.coli. Salmonella. That sort of thing and not in the same area. One in Oregon. Florida. Yeah. Floridas great for explosions. Boats always catching fire and blowing up. Drunken accidents. Or Cubans, pro or anti Castro. And Colombians. Those goddamn drug dealers are always killing each other. Easy enough to make it look like a drug hit. How long can it take me to learn how to make a little plastique? Sure as hell dont need tons of explosives like those animals in Oklahoma City. Or letter bombs. Can probably figure out how to make a small delivery system for a little plastique. Nothing fancy. Wood. Cant be detected. No rush. One here, one later. Have plenty of time. Can even get a few mafiosi. Make it look like it was another mafioso. Start a war and have those greaseballs shooting each other. Should be simple.

Start with the VA. Its loaded with pricks who need killing. Though killings too good for some of them. They should be tortured the way theyve tortured millions of helpless guys. Krist, what a bunch of rotten scumbags. Better do that out on the coast. No point in having them hunting around here. Can take in some HMO bastards too. It feels good just thinking about it.

Finally got it. He was true to his word, said it would only be a few days, and he was right. Hmm…couple of days… Miraculous…perhaps mystical days. So much changed in those days. How extraordinary…the change…yes, definitely mystical and miraculous. I would have killed the wrong person. Getting even with the real culprits by killing myself and blaming them is truly madness. If there must be killing, then let it be appropriate. Killing myself is tantamount to murder…the execution of an innocent individual…at best the accidental killing of an innocent bystander. I am certainly not the one who needs killing simply because I could find no purpose to my life. How unbelievably extraordinary the change in just a few days. Remarkable. I dont think the magnitude of the change has as yet fully registered. Will take time to fully assimilate, to see my past state of hopelessness clearly. Perhaps, even with time, it will be as simple as it appears to be now: my life had no meaning. How far can money and cars and homes and all the other toys take you? There must be something of substance in a persons life, a reason to get up, to wash, to dress, to eat, to look at the day, mingle with people, do whats needed. A person must contribute to the world in some way or life is worse than meaningless…its…yeah, I guess its nothing more than an obscene joke. Yeah, but whos laughing? Yes indeed, the laborer is worthy of his hire and peace of mind and the joy of living are the worthy result of a life of service…a life well-lived… Hmmm, yes, yes indeed, truly a fortuitous glitch in the system… Life is truly a wonder…

Wonder how you buy an illegal handgun? They say theres thousands, hundreds of thousands floating around the streets. Who knows? Got to know all about this one before I worry about more. When I know all about this one and feel really comfortable with it, I/ll probably be able to nose out some gun sellers. I/ll intuitively know where they are, or recognize them. Thats usually how these things work. But first Ive got to do what that guy said and go to a range and get familiar with it. Learn to shoot it and take it apart and clean it and all that. In the army those guys learn how to take their weapons apart blindfolded…and put them back together again. Just take my time. Dont rush. Plenty of time. Plenty of time now that I know what to do with my time…

Yeah, taking my times paid off. Pretty good shot. Good enough for my purposes. And I can take this apart and put it together with my eyes closed. Got to stay nice and calm. No more getting excited and angry. As a matter of fact I no longer feel angry. Dont want to kill myself either. Now I know who needs killing, and its not me. So

I/ll stay nice and calm…focused. Yeah, thats the secret, staying focused and not dissipating my energies with anger. I/ll simply continue to download the info I need—my god, what a great tool the Internet is. There really is everything on it. Nice and steady…and calm.

But it would be nice to strangle that son of a bitch Barnard at the VA, to just wait for him some night and force him to drive out of town and slowly choke the bastard…oh just thinking of my hands around his throat is so sweet—No! No! Cant allow that. This is not going to be some sort of ego trip. Insane to go to prison, or even be killed, for eliminating a parasite like Barnard. Nice and calm and never be noticed. If he dies from food poisoning how can I possibly be implicated or incriminated? No leaving a record for posterity, or even plans or notes. Everything destroyed as soon as possible. No manifestos. Now theres real madness. As if killing a couple of people is going to change the basic structure/foundation of this world. No crusade for the betterment of mankind… Ach, betterment of mankind. What drivel…what rubbish. All animals. Some just bigger than others. But everyone is always looking for someone to push around, someone lower on the food chain. Someone to feel superior to. And if you cant do it at work then do it at home. Thats the beauty of having a family. A wife to slap around, kids to punish and whip. Seems like the only reason people get married is to have someone they can abuse in private, undetected. Especially those christians! Boy, do they love to punish. Whip their ass! Yeah, lets have a party. Dont forget to invite the children there I go again. Cant do that. Dont want to get too personal. No causes. Just a quiet, simple, satisfying way to get back at this world for suffocating me, for crushing me, for trying to kill my spirit. But they havent and they wont. They came close. Oh they came close. Was all set to put a gun in my mouth and pull the trigger. But there was a computer glitch. Isnt that something? A stupid glitch and I had to wait a few days and then I saw the errors of my ways, saw so clearly that I was killing the wrong person. Its not me that needs killing, its them. Funny how things can change in the wink of an eye.

...yeah, E.coli is the best way to go. Other food poisonings too difficult and sort of specialized. And nobody would think it could be deliberate, not with all the outbreaks we/ve had these last years...and it should be easy... *Eating meat, especially ground beef, that has not been cooked sufficiently to kill E.coli can cause infection. Contaminated meat looks and smells normal. Although the number of organisms required to cause disease is not known, it is suspected to be very small.*

Very small. Wonder if the CIA has ever used this for...*elimination*? Maybe they should have tried that instead of cigars with Castro. Then we wouldnt have to live in constant fear of being invaded by the forces of communism only 90 miles away... We will fight them on the beaches, we will fight them in the streets, we will fight them in the book depository—OOPS, we fucked up there. Oh well, as long as they dont get to Wall Street everything is fine. What fools…we couldve sued the Cuban cigar makers for billions of dollars. Wonder if some enterprising legal beagle has already thought of that and is waiting for 'normal relations' between us. Normal relations? Guess that means face to face. Yuck…that sounds disgusting. All that hair and garlic breath…sounds revolting…to coin a phrase. Enough, enough. Back to work.

So… E.coli/s the way to go, and rotten beef is a source. Suppose I could go into any McDonalds and play Russian roulette with hamburgers. Maybe thats the attraction for fast food joints, the excitement, the adrenaline rush from not knowing if this is your last meal—Okay, okay, calm down. Lets browse the Net some more and see…

Now thats interesting…*unpasteurized apple juice*…unpasteurized apple juice. Hmmm…wonder which way is better???? Which way??? What the hell, use them both. I/ll just make a little apple juice and drop some ground beef into it, put it in the sun and see what it grows. Yeah…thats simple enough… Hmmm, how will I know if Ive actually grown the bacteria? Good question. Oh no, one thing I cant do is test it on some kitty cat or stray dog. Or any creature, really… No, not even a mouse or a rat. If I could capture one of those ugly street rats, but how in the hell would I do that? And Im certainly not going to go to a pet shop and buy one, cage and all. Jesus, just keep feeding it a little beef and apple juice and see what happens? No thanks, Im not a ghoul. If I could do that I could get a job with some drug company and torture rabbits and mice and monkeys and god knows how many other creatures. How can they do that? Sever their vocal chords so you cant hear them crying with pain and just keep torturing them and go home at the end of the day, eat, relax, sleep, get up in the morning and do it all over again. Day after day. I suppose theyre 'just doing their job'. Maybe I/ll just have to let it cook for a while then see if it does the job. I dont know, that doesnt seem like a smart approach. Could go on for ever. There must be some way without hurting some poor little critter, there—wait a second. All those reports I was reading about outbreaks in drinking water, they obviously were able to test the water so there must be test kits available. People are always testing for something. Lets get back on the Net here and see what we got... Yeah...yeah, that sounds good...no, not that one, none where you send in a sample with your name and address. Who knows what the laws may be. They come up with a sample loaded with E.coli and they may have to call the Board of Health or something. Yeah, thered be some government agency involved. I can just see it, men dressed in black, faces hidden behind black veils and sun glasses, knocking at the door. Whos there? The E.coli death squad. Oh do come in. Yeah, sure, that would be a good way to remain anonymous. We can forget those firms. Looks like the best are the Water Testing Kits 'guaranteed to detect contaminates, including bacteria'... Yeah...they should be worth a shot. Okay, lets get them ordered and get on with it. This apple juice ground beef combo should be cookin by the time they get here. Maybe I can sell the idea to McDonalds. A new Macbeefapple… Hey, wait a minute, they can freeze it and sell it as a 'quick snack popsicle'. A real winner, a million dollar idea. God only knows where we can go with this—Enough! Enough! Time for frivolity later, after the work has been done. Still a lot of work left to do. I culture it…then I have to transport it and deliver the package…to coin a phrase. Have to find a safe way to get it from here to there. Evidently it wont take much. Especially if its potent. And it should be a hell of a lot more potent than a hamburger or glass of apple juice. And its not detectable by taste. Obviously. Just as obviously food poisoning should be in food, so the best 'delivery system' is food…lunch time. Okay, have to 'first things first' this. Have to make certain he eats in that coffee shop each day. Just because I happened to notice him in there once at the salad bar doesnt mean he goes there every day. Have to check that out, be absolutely certain. Cant determine how to deliver a little food additive without knowing exactly where he/ll be. But for now I can have a tentative plan based on the distinct possibility that he does eat there at least once a week. I remember he was at the salad bar…which may not be too important. The image I have really clearly in my mind is a large container of soda…yeah, with ice cubes clinking around in it…ice cold soda…the logical 'receptacle'. Get a belly full of soda and E.c in his nice warm tummy and it should do wonders for his health. Oh yes indeedy do. Alright, no tangents, not now. Keep focused. Have to get the 'culture' from here to there. Okay…now lets break it down. If I really can grow the bacteria in my little brew, it will be extremely virulent…yeah, so it wont take much. All I have to do is bring a couple of ounces. That should do it. Probably a lot less will do…yeah, but it should be just as easy to get 2 ounces in that soda as one and the more the merrier…to coin a phrase. But suppose it leaks or spills over me??? Shit! Cant wear surgical gloves and green scrubs, that—wait a second, what the hell am I talking about? Its not going to do me anything if it touches my skin for gods sake. It has to be ingested. Any old bottle with a tight cap will do just as long as its small enough to hold in one hand and dump the contents into that cup without being noticed. Yeah, thats important. Well maybe not. Even if someone notices me with a little bottle who is going to associate that with someone dying from E.coli poisoning? Even if they do hear of it. No, no, a case of a purloined letter. Simply look and act like anyone else in there and no one will remember. A little misdirection will help. Yeah, reach in a different direction with one hand while the other drops the E.c in the cup. Better practice that. Yeah, be able to do it with my eyes closed just like taking the gun apart and reassembling it blindfolded. Train the body. If the mind bogs down with fear the body can still do what it has to do. Yeah… Okay. So, where am I? Two ounce bottle. Any bottle. Wont be seen, hopefully, so something that fits easily in the palm of my hand and is easy to open while concealed. Actually, any old bottle will do. Have to keep this simple. Nothing fancy. So, where am I? Got my culture cooking and by the time the test kits get here it should be done. And I/ll know what hes up to and everything will be ready. In the meantime better get some work done. Funny, been making a living with computers for years, and love them, but this is the first time Ive had so much fun. This goes so much beyond making a living. This truly makes living worthwhile. Oh I love you, love you, my little sweetheart. What was that old phone ad, something like, Reach out and touch somebody today, or tell them you love them, or some such thing? Whatever. But we will reach out and kill some one. Yes in deed. Someone who truly deserves it...who needs it. Or at least the rest of the world does. Okay, enough of that. Just relax, get some work done, and tomorrow we take the next step in our little endeavor.

...well, one thing I know I wont be doing is parking in the parking lot. God only knows how many different disasters could occur (dis *ass* ter? hell, damn near killed her), and too easy to shut down the exits, not that there should be any reason for that, Im not going in there with an arm load of automatic weapons. This is a Federal Building, not a high school. But there—enough of this negativity. This is simply a reconnaissance mission, a simple fact finding endeavor. This seems like the best place to park, but think I/ll cruise around, circle the block, make sure Im familiar with the area, dont want to take anything for granted... Not too much traffic down here, a simple drive. But Im not making a getaway from a bank robbery. Just fitting in, thats all, just fitting in with my surroundings. Dont want to get too dramatic or James Bondish about this. Sure as hell dont need histrionics. No cops and robbers or spies in from the cold. No shooting it out with coppers and making it to the top of the world…

Okay, this is the best place to park. Simple access to the area. Yeah…good… So, here we go, a simple stroll along the ugly Federal Property. I guess all governments, at all levels, want you to know youre on government property by making it, at the very least, unattractive. Its incredible, as soon as youre out of the government area the streets are tree lined and shady, birds sing, everything looks, sounds and feels peaceful, then one more step and youre approaching the pits of hell. There should be a huge sign: Abandon hope all who enter here. No, no, no, not getting into that right now. Just a short, simple stroll to the coffee shop, taking in everything, every little turn and corner, all possible routes to the car. What time is it??? 12:10. A good time. Probably takes the same lunch hour every day, so if hes here now we/ll know.

Wow, they really keep it cool in here. Guess they sell more food that way. Well, hes not here now… Best to wait a few minutes to be sure he doesnt show up soon…yeah, I did overlook that. They may stagger lunch hours on a half hour basis. But that wouldnt have anything to do with him, being the head of this whole rotten VA mess. He probably does what he wants on the job just as he does with the vets…screwem. Probably goes out as late as he can to make the afternoon go faster. Have to rest after a tiring day of destroying lives. Hey, dont knock it, its not as easy as it looks to be a scumbag and—Enough. Keep focused! If you cant do it now what will you do on D-Day? Time to take another stroll. Dont want to just hang around here looking conspicuous and obvious. Use the time to check out the rest of the area. Dont want any sudden surprises.

Whup, theres the heat. Everyones trying to stay in the narrow strip of shade from the building. Amazing how theyre afraid of the sunlight. Weaving in and out. What the hell. Just take it nice and easy. Wonder how much good those barriers do? Cant get a vehicle close to the building, but I guess someone can still create a gigantic mess. No repetition of Oklahoma City though. Jesus, that was a real nutcase. All those people…and children…people who had nothing to do with what ever in the hell he was pissed off about. Blind, bloodthirsty stupidity. Absolutely senseless. Didnt come close to getting anyone even vaguely responsible for whatever pissed him off. Thats the problem with blind hatred…it defeats itself. All those people dead, hes dead, and nothing accomplished. Emotionalism. A killer. Must remain calm and detached. And remain anonymous. No ego trips, just attaining the desired results. Wonder how many people there are walking free with mountainous amounts of money in a Swiss bank account, or some off-shore bank, who have quietly stolen millions and just faded from sight. Anonymous. Yes… Ha ha, yeah, posterity. I guess some people are so desperate, feel so insignificant, that they will do anything to find a place in history. The key is to do a good job and let that be its own reward. No posing in front of cameras. No fanatical declarations of justice or whatever nonsense the current crop of crazies are spewing forth at any particular time. Screwem. Let them eat cake…

Ahhh, that cool air does feel good. Guess I did get a bit warm walking around in the sun… Lets see—yeah, there he is, good old Barnard. Salad, coke, and pie. I bet its diet coke too. A bowl of rabbit food, a diet coke, and a nice big piece of apple pie. Good thinking, watching his calories…lets see what size cup he has…hmmmm, yeah, definitely a large one. It figures… Well, lets see…yeah, get a cup of water, sit for a moment, then, as they say in Bellevue, Im off.

Now, if I had dropped my little kiss of death in his coke—hey, I like that—this is the route I would be taking back to the car. Just a leisurely pace, sipping my cup of water, melting into the surroundings, just another worker among workers walking to his car… Yeah…come back tomorrow for a repeat performance. Get used to this path. Do it with my eyes closed. Except the driving. Okay, okay, a jokes a joke, but Ive got to stop these stupid puns. Must stay focused. Focused…

Okay, key in the ignition, seat belt—jesus, wouldnt that be something, get stopped by the police for not wearing a seat belt, panic, and give yourself away. Its happened, Im sure. Big thing is to just act normal, nothing to attract attention. Use directional, pull away from curb, merge into traffic, a car among cars…and go home…

So, simple enough. Go through it again tomorrow. Yeah, now I have to practice dumping the culture in his coke. Lets see…yeah, the table is about the height of the railings for the trays. So, his cup would be about…here…yeah, thats about right, and I/d be next to him and reach over so my other hand is hidden and quickly dump it in. Yeah, that was easy enough. No one will see this little bottle in my hand… Hmmm, it is possible his cup may be filled up so high there wont be enough room… yeah, important. Seems to me he always takes a drink right after he fills the cup, but better make sure tomorrow. Cant let some little thing like this ruin everything. No. Anyway, in the meantime I can continue practicing dumping the culture in his cup. Seems simple so far. Havent spilled a drop. Sure no one can see the bottle in—should walk with it to be sure it wont spill…take a look in the mirror…lets see… Nothing…no matter what angle, nothing…nope, nothing. Hmmm, good idea, bring the bottle tomorrow with plain water and see if Im right. Yeah, like that.

Okay, park here. Looks like theres always places here, just like yesterday. Fine, just go through the drill.

… Yeah, I was right, he does take a drink right away. Aware of more than I realize. Okay, time to concentrate…get behind him on line, slide my tray carefully and wait……okay, now reach over to other side and dump…and stroll away…put the tray on the pile, and slowly leave, no hurry, going back to work and who wants to hurry back to work, just stroll out the door…same walk, same routine, same drill…

god,

just a dry run and my heart is pounding. It went perfectly. Not a hitch, not a drop spilled. Details, details. Pay attention to details. Its all in the details. Yeah…youre right, this is going to work. I can feel it in my bones. It is going to work. Keep practicing. No complacency. By the time the culture is ready, I/ll truly be fine tuned like a violin…or a racing car. Always the details.

Well, according to this tester theres enough E.coli in this culture to take care of half the city. Well, theres no reason why we cant take care of Barnard tomorrow.

Someone elses error gave me the time to see mine. Providence?

Okay, time to start. Ive tracked that prick Barnard long enough. Time to review, a check list. Culture is virulent, more than ready. Bottle is ready. Know where to park. Can empty my bottle in his coke with my eyes closed. Can walk the route from the lunch room to the car with my eyes closed. Everything has been tested and retested. I am ready. Better do it now. Dont want to over train and become stiff and inflexible. Must remain loose and focused on the process. Fascinating…absolutely fascinating. Feel like any moment now I/ll be so focused on the process that I/ll become a part of it and just flow through the ether and become a part of every atom, every proton and quark and resonate through out the Universe...all of it...all, all... Who knows, perhaps some day it will come to pass. Oh, what a sublime thought, to float free of the body and mind, just a pulse in space...but it would be *my* pulse, *my* awareness, awareness of freedom, free from the vice-like oppression that has crushed me all my life and guys like Barnard who are forever frustrating me, torturing me, letting me get just so far then slamming the door in my face, forcing me to struggle just to prove I deserve my daily bread, god what animals these people are, worse than the goddamn mafia, at least theyre out and out thieves and murderers, but these others always pretend theyre your friend, here to help us—help us! help us go crazy. They know I deserve those benefits and they just keep turning me down for no reason at all, no justifiable reason and I have to prove over and over that I—ahhh, the hell with it. Im tired of all this madness. Tomorrow I/ll give him a little taste of what hes been serving. After tomorrow he/ll never frustrate me again. And I/ll not get careless. Now that I have a true purpose to life I have no worry about my mind not staying focused. Its almost too easy. He doesnt know me from Adam. He doesnt even know my name. All he knows is that another form letter is going out over his signature denying benefits. Perhaps I should bump into him and smile—no, no, none of that. No bravado, no silly games. Keep focused and remain as inconspicuous, as anonymous as possible. Nothing out of the ordinary. Take nothing for granted. I wonder what it will be like? I can feel my stomach fluttering just thinking about it. Ive never killed anyone like this, not that its really killing, I mean its no different than a war, but this is different than those killers too, its not like Im some kind of professional assassin. Not at all. Merely a spokesman for thc oppressed, a mere conduit for a micro-organism…yeah, thats right, yeah, only a conduit, an ambassador so to speak. But will I be able to do it? God, my bowels are rumbling just thinking about it. I/ll be alright. Its him or me. Thats what it comes down to, him or me, and better him. No, I dont care if he has a family. They deserve what they get. They must be just like him, or will be. He doesnt care if we have families or not, if our children suffer because he enjoys torturing us, enjoys refusing our claims. The greatest joy of his life is making certain we do not get what we have worked for and deserve. I can just see him coming home at night and telling his wife and children how many veterans disability claims he turned down today, and how proud they are of him. Youre damned right I dont feel sorry for them any more than they feel sorry for us. In a sense you can say Im simply doing what hes been doing all these years, Im rejecting his claim. Ha ha, thats a good one, I like that, rejecting his claim.

Enough. Ive got to stop all this rambling and meandering. Need to relax and get a good nights sleep. I definitely do not want to be groggy tomorrow. Must have my wits about me. So… A nice warm bath, a glass of warm milk, and to bed.

The man lies on his side, facing away from the window, so the light has yet to penetrate his closed lids, only an ear and part of a cheek visible so it is not certain, certainly not by whatever expression there may be on his face, if his sleep is peaceful and dreamless, yet it would seem there can be no nightmares, even though his decision of the night before, and the events that are ahead of him this day, are, to say the least, momentous. How many times is the question Can I kill him? turning itself around in his mind? Can he, in the safety of sleep, reply: I am not killing him, E.coli is? His face is still not visible, yet there are significant twitchings in his body, perhaps unnoticeable to an untrained eye, yet clearly apparent, twitchings that indicate that all is not peaceful, that there is an ever increasing activity in his mind, an activity not unknown to many. The room grows brighter and brighter and the light eases itself through his eyelids and soon he will be awake and not concern himself with what may have happened while he slept but most certainly will concentrate on the day before him, a day that will be momentous no matter what he may elect to do.

Guess its a nice day out there. Bright in here. Can feel it on my lids. Seems a little heavy. Keeps shutting my eyes. Well…have to open them sooner or later. Have plenty of time. All morning. Feel a little tired, a bit sluggish. Shower will take care of that. Okay. Just pop them open and sit up.

There you go. Better get in the shower.

Oh god, that feels good. Wonder who invented the shower? A stroke of pure genius. It turns the whole day around. Always feel better after a shower. No matter how rotten you feel when you get up. Always. Seem to feel pretty good anyway. Just another day. Surprised Im so relaxed, guess I expected to be a little tense, sort of uptight… I dont know, maybe kinda worried about this whole thing. It is a big day. It really is a big deal. Dont feel that way though. Well, you know this isnt a spur of the moment action. A lot of work and research, a lot of research and pin point planning have gone into this endeavor, so you see its not surprising Im relaxed. Sit back and enjoy the morning and save my energy for this afternoon. Oh, I do know what Im doing, you can bet on that…

As a matter of fact it is extraordinary how relaxed I am. Wont be long I/ll be leaving and seeing gods gift to the VA and wishing him *bon appetit*, wonder if he/ll get a pain in the gut, O krist I hope so. A little poetic justice. At least that. Cant choke him…well, could probably get away with it. People get caught because theyre stupid…or nutcases. They dont stay focused. Some dont even have a plan. Just like to kill people. Advertise their guilt. Too much evidence all over. Dumb psycho business of wanting to get caught. Or the obvious connection. They check the files for people who want to kill Barnard theyd find thousands, thousands…hundreds of thousands. Hey, natural causes. Contaminated food. Cant get caught. No crime. Should get there early. Park the car close, not too close. Easy walk to the coffee shop. Bad idea to get there too early. Hang around and some one gets paranoid and calls the cops. Planning always pays off. Guess thats why Im so relaxed. Nice and easy. Just drive normally, walk normally. No big thing. Just another day.

Traffics not too bad. Maybe most of the crazies stayed home today. Not too bad a drive. Going west this time of day helps. Traffics bad enough without the sun blinding you. Amazing lack of self consciousness. Dont feel like I have to watch every car. Just keep alert. Stay in the right lane and always yield the right of way. It always amazes me how inconsiderate most drivers are. A little common courtesy would prevent 90% of the accidents. Just let the other guy have the right of way. Krist, youd think their lives depended on getting ahead of everyone. Weave in and out, cut people off and for gods sake dont use your directionals, whatever you do dont signal you dumb son of a bitch, just wander back and forth, zip across 10 lanes of traffic, thats fine, maybe cause a few accidents, even kill a few people, but what the hell, you own the fucking street so you can do what in the hell you want and whatever you do, dont go to all the trouble of pushing the lever up or down, please, please, I know it takes too much energy so dont bother, please, dont bother just go your merry way and dont fucking signal you numb nuts son of a bitch jesus krist common courtesy is ancient history with these maniacs, love to just ram one of those bastards sometime, just plow right into him then go my merry way with my finger extended toward the heavens and send a few of these bastards to hell, god I hate these creepy bastards, oh shit, I have to get over to make a left, you son of a bitch, why cant you let me in you miserable prick god how I hate them, they can see Im trying to get over what the hell do you think that blinker means, the car has palsy fuckem, I/ll just stay right here until someone lets me in, let them honk all they want I dont give a shit how far back traffic is blocked Im—thanks, thanks, krist, why couldnt someone have done that a half hour ago well fuck them all, krist, they got me all fucked up, my heads spinning and it looks like theres no place to park on this rotten street, oh shit, what the fuck am I gonna do drive up and down the street until I find something or attract the attention of a cop, goddamn it, cant park in the lot, just cant take that chance, have to be able to get to the car and just drive away, not get caught in some fucking traffic jam in the lot because some asshole is going the wrong way or, oh, thank krist, that guys getting out, in the shade too, dont need a boiling hot car from sitting in the sun, not today, what time, oh I have more than 20 minutes oh shit, I feel all fucked up just because of those asshole drivers, oh fuck, wheres the bottle, what happened, I had it oh, here it is, better sit here for a minute, cant even see straight oh shit this better—cant get all fucked up because of those shit heads, I just cant, I cant postpone it, cant do that, it/ll spook everything, have to just relax, oh god, my fucking stomach is knotted and cramped, I think I have to shit, oh no, this cant be happening, its killing me, have to move, have to get my legs to move, cant sit here any longer, have to get going, have to oh shit almost opened the door in front of that car, jesus, my heart is pounding all over my chest and clogging my throat, this is insane, I was doing so well until those assholes…gotta breathe, nice and slow…in…out…in…out…

okay, can open the door now, just walk nice and slow oh shit, gotta lock the goddamn thing. Thats all I need, come back here and the cars gone, stolen by one of those low lifes. Okay, theres no need to rush. Nice and slow. Just sort of saunter to the coffee shop. Breathe slowly, walk slowly. Stay alert. Just stroll. Going to meet a friend and have a little lunch. No big deal. Slow. The sweats burning my eyes. Stand in the shade a minute. Im soaking wet. How did I get so wet? Breathe. Slow… Slow…

The man stands in the shade of a building. A tall building. The work home for thousands. Tall enough to cast a shadow the man is grateful for, a long shadow that stretches to the flower beds. He wipes at the sweat with a handkerchief, but there is no cooling breeze so the sweat continually replaces itself. But it does lessen. It does not drip from his face, it is simply moisture oozing from his pores. He attempts to regard his body in a window to see if it looks as wet as it feels. He doesnt want to be obvious so his attempts are not overly successful. As best as he can determine by looking sideway in the glass while doing all possible to appear to be inspecting the sky, he gives the impression of being dry. Is this important? Apparently he believes so. He is concerned with not looking overheated and thus conspicuous. He still remembers to be aware of his breathing, to breathe slowly, to appear relaxed. He places his wet handkerchief in his rear pocket and slides his hands in his front pockets to dry them. This is of the utmost importance. What folly it would be to have the bottle slide from his hand because it is wet. A fiasco of monumental proportions. It is almost time to enter the coffee shop. He appears frozen in the heat. He forces his body to turn, however slightly, then turns his head.

Oh my god, there he is…hes going into the coffee shop

The man is rigid. Stiff beyond recognition. A piece of statuary. It appears his heart is pounding at his chest, seeking freedom from the confines of its home. An eternal moment. Truly. How strange that people are still walking, birds still flying. Is everyone, and everything, unaware that time is standing still, it, too, frozen in the heat?

O krist, I feel like Im going to faint. What in the hell is this, Ive got to move but my legs are so fucking weak, think Im going to fall if I move. I cant do this. I cant go through with it. I didnt expect this. Somethings choking off my air everythings going around in circles. Cant get my legs to work oh god, think Im gonna puke and shit my pants. Its not supposed to be like this. Im just supposed to dump the culture in his coke and go home. Its not supposed to be a big deal. I mean, nothing might happen. Might not even get sick. I dont know if I did a good job on the E.coli culture. How do I know those test kits are accurate? Would think two wouldnt be wrong. Both the same reading…more or less. Just have to assume the tests are accurate, that the culture is deadly. Followed all the directions. Oh god. Let me get inside, out of the heat. Just lean against the window and slide around the corner to the door. That son of a bitch is at the salad bar like nothings going on. Hes fucking oblivious. What the fuck does he care how many people he fucks over. Doesnt give it a fucking thought. Well youre gonna give something some thought scumbag because this is going to be your last meal, oh that cold air feels good. Wow, like a slap in the face. Thats all that was wrong. Too hot. Yeah. Feel much better. Yeah, I/ll just stand here a minute, catch my breath, and just ease my way over toward him, come up from behind...just nice and slow and steady oh god, I cant believe Im really going to do this oh jesus, there go my legs and my stomach, oh shit, not again, I cant let this happen, I cant let this rotten son of bitch get away with it, I just cant, I dont care how dizzy I am, oh god, help me, help me get it in his coke, only a few more feet, the bottles ready jesus my hands all wet o krist I shouldve wrapped it in tape jesus Im trembling so much I can hardly see, I/ll have to hold it with two hands, o krist I cant do it, I cant...okay, relax, relax...in...out...in...out... okay, everythings fine, his coke is right there, plenty of room, almost half empty, just reach over toward the beets...dump it in, thats it, nothing to it, done, done, just pick up your tray and move, just keep moving, have to keep these legs moving, keep moving, keep moving, for krists sake dont stop now, dont look around, just keep moving, toward the door, its getting closer and closer, just keep moving, getting closer no, dont look behind you, keep moving, toward the door, ahhh, just a shove yeah, out, out, nice and warm, oh that feels good, nice and warm, shivering stops, just needed to be in the warmth and keep moving, for krists sake dont panic, dont run, nice and easy, remember how you walked before, just strolling, hands in your pockets and stroll, feel the warmth of the sun, oh how good that feels, gets right to the marrow of your bones, dont look back, move your head, be normal, but dont look back, nice and easy, feel the sun on your face, oh great, dont hear anything, no commotion, he didnt notice a thing, just kept piling food on his plate, just keep strolling, beautiful day, jesus, Im so excited feels like my chest is going to explode, feels like Ive been hit with a bat, or pounded by Ali, I/ll never make it to the car, krist I have to sit soon, getting wobbly again, got a real cotton mouth oh shit, I walked right past the car, okay, okay, no panic, we/ll just turn around and go back, take a look and see if…no, no activity, just usual people traffic, everythings okay, just get in the car, damn cant get the fucking key in the lock, oh god, okay, okay, nice and easy, there, open the door slowly, nice and slowly, ease into the car, now breathe in…breathe out…breathe in…breathe out…thats it nice and slow, just relax, nice and easy, have to get going, cant sit here too long, looks suspicious…take small side streets, slowly, carefully oh god, I cant get the key what in the hells wrong with this o krist I cant make it get in the lock you rotten get in there oh god the steering wheel feels good on my forehead maybe I can just sit here like this for a while with my eyes closed and catch my breath Im shaking so much I cant see straight oh no gotta sit up someone sees me like this theyre liable to think Ive had a heart attack or something just have to get out of here oh shit I cant see, everythings fogged up damn what the hells going on just take it easy, comeon breathe…yeah breathe…okay can see where Im going nice and slow people get pissed off because Im going slow the hell withem…but I cant, cant attract attention have to get to the side streets, just hold on a few more blocks nice and easy the seat belt gotta get that on oh shit get in there o krist I hope some kid doesnt come running out in front of the car those crazy skateboarders are everywhere or a cat they go crazy sometimes and run right at the car oh please no kids no cats no kids no birds no nothing just have to get home oh great lots of trees on this block and no traffic makes it so much easier no sun blaring off glass or metal watch out for the stop signs no rolling stops just stop then go and always courteous, must always drive courteously oh what a great street a life saver wonder if they are right and you cant taste it cant think of that now got to get home in one piece just be careful of the light flicking off the leaves dont get distracted

by all means do not get distracted. The possible events that can occur in the wink of an eye are endless, absolutely endless. So though he is more than three quarters of the way home, has, in fact, only a few more streets to drive, about ten actually, still the possibilities for disaster are legion. Yet it does look, more and more, as if he will arrive at his home without incident. Even now he is parking the car. Yet he does not get out but sits staring through the windshield. He is, perhaps, uncertain if his legs will support his weight if he stands. He looks around carefully before opening the door wanting, I am certain, to avoid the ultimate irony of thrusting open his door and stepping in front of a vehicle and...and what? Who knows? But there is no traffic, yet he does have to lean against the car adjusting to standing, until his vision clears and he can walk slowly and carefully up the walk.

My god! the walk looks endless. How can the door be so far away? It looks like its in another land. How can I possibly make it to the door, its much too far. I just cant do it. But I cant stand here forever—the longest journey starts with a single step—have to get off the street. Just push myself off the car. One foot, then the other, thats all, one foot, then the other, over and over, cant walk too fast anyway, feel wobbly, something wrong with my balance, god, the neighbors will think Im drunk if I keep staggering and what will they think if I fall that I had a heart attack and call 911 no, have to keep my balance and just get to the door but I cant look desperate god only knows whos watching me have to look relaxed like Im just strolling up the walk, thats it, look around at the trees up at the sky stop and look at a flower, look really interested and get my wind feel like Ive run a couple of miles maybe I can whistle or puff my cheeks like I am so if they are watching theyll think Im just strolling and whistling and enjoying the birds and the flowers o krist Ive got to get to that door and in the house jesus now the sweat is running into my eyes and I cant see cant take out my handkerchief, too obvious, just pretend Im scratching my head and wipe my eyes with my finger tip oh that feels good can see just a few more feet oh sweet jesus Im going to make it nice and easy key in the lock just sort of lean against the door I think thats how I usually open it I think roll behind it and push it closed I made it I made it the door is locked shut Im home I wonder what time it is how long have I been away I cant remember what time I left the coffee shop never knew really have to sit oh god that feels good should take my jacket off and tie cant bother have to sit rest oh god I feel faint whats going on????

Oh thats better, much better. Catch my breath. Wow that feels good! How did I ever breathe with the collar buttoned? No wonder I felt faint, I was being strangled. Feel a million times better just opening it. Get this jacket off in a minute…or two. That air feels so good, just going right down my throat. Cant believe how different my chest feels. Legs still wobbly. Damn. Why in the hell cant I stand? Getting dizzy just from trying to stand. This is crazy for krists—okay, just relax. Sit a few more minutes. No rush. Nice and easy. Damn. Not even 3 oclock. Seems like years ago. Just a few hours. He goes to lunch at one. Cant seem to remember what happened. Can see it, but memorys hazy. How strange. Know exactly what happened, yet… At least I think I know what happened. Could I be wrong? Cant be. No. Howd I get out? The coffee shop. Didnt run. No. To the car. Cant remember. But I drove home. Im here. How in the name of krist did I make it? All the way? I dont remember it yeah, thats right, my eyes burned. Sweat. Five miles. At least. Should remember something. Wonder if I can stand now? Think Im soaking wet. No, better not shower. Legs too wobbly.

Krist, Im really home. I did it. Didnt I? Yeah, I know, but better check the bottle. At least that way—Empty. Knew I dumped it. I really did it. I did it…and Im here. Home. All the way home. Wonder if the cars okay? Didnt hit anything. O krist, I/d remember something like that. Sure. Yeah!!!! Im here. Its over—Hey! Im standing. My legs are fine. Pick up your pallet and walk my son. Maybe tomorrow I/ll remember more clearly. A shower. Hot. Cold. Get these clothes off. What a great day. Greatest day of my life. No, no tossing clothes on the bed. Hang up the suit, nice and tidy. Everything in perfect order.

Indeed, all is perfect in the perfectly ordered life of the man…at this particular moment. Our man is singing in the shower, his legs sturdy, the water hot, relaxing, mist filling the bathroom, clinging to the mirror. In time, perhaps soon, he will increase the cold water in small increments and when he finally turns off the water he will feel invigorated and rub himself briskly and step forth a new man, at least for a moment.

Bring me giants! Cant believe my legs were so weak just a few minutes ago. I could climb a mountain. No, I could run up the son of a bitch. God, Im starving. Ha ha, no wonder, I didnt eat any lunch. Whip something up. Roast beef sandwich and a beer sounds good. Pickle too. Sounds great. Watch a movie while I eat. Could go out later to a restaurant and celebrate with a late dinner. Nice piece of broiled fish I havent checked the car. I know nothings wrong but better check it anyway no point in taking chances well I dont know what chances but its the little details that make or break you no I wont look conspicuous Im not going to stare at every inch I/ll just walk slowly around to the drivers side yeah thats it look carefully no rush open the door yeah open the door and lean in and op—no get in and open the glove box and rummage around for a minute now get out and walk around the other way. . . yeah, who is going to notice just go back up the walk nice and easy and get back in my chair and finish my sandwich, nothing to it, and my legs feel fine, didnt wobble not even for a minute. Strong as a running backs. Still afternoon. Cant seem to get used to the time. Seems like such a long day. Guess it is but still plenty of time. What a wonder this day is and—maybe I should hide the bottle dont want a series of coincidences revealing what happened but what can be revealed still you cant be too safe but if some weird set of circumstances leads to the bottle what can be more oh for crying out loud, just throw it all away, bottle, culture all of it, but if I need more oh this is silly, I can always make more and what would I say if the cops found the jar of culture in the closet okay, lets stop this, forget all this, no one is going to be looking for anything throw everything out and sit here and relax and listen to the birds, yeah talk to me, no sing to me my finches and mockingbirds, yes sing such lovely songs my pretty birds pretty birds sing sing how sweet your song a song so light and delicate a lullaby that puts the devil to sleep ah yes defenseless against a microbe how sweetly poetic like the nightingale to undo the tyranny of demons with something invisible to the naked eye oh yes the demonic eye is naked to my scrutiny I will seek you out uncover you and lay waste to you without your knowledge without your knowing that you are being sent to the fires of your own creation still unaware of my existence not even a name or face to you not even the 9 digits of a social security number unaware this entity you chose to treat with contempt is your executioner oh yes I will eat cake while you eat the dirt of your grave oh lets hope your pain is severe the least life can do to avenge all those thousands you have caused such egregious pain to oh lets hope the agony brings moans and pleas from your lips sweet music to join the singing of my nightingale sweet songs to celebrate the worms crawling through your loathsome carcass

What a lovely evening—night? no its still evening, hard to tell this time of year, wonder what time it is oh not important, lots of people on the street, wonder if I should get something to eat oh not now maybe later dont think Im hungry, damn cant remember where Ive been I mean I know where Ive been just cant remember being there I really do remember the streets of course I can…lets see theres Lawrence then Hobbs th—well yes of course theres Selby but I live there naturally I didnt start with that thinking of the streets later okay so theres Selby, Bankcroft, then Lawrence I know but thats just a short little piece of a street just a 'bridge' really from Bankcroft to Lawrence okay okay so Solo Court, Lawrence, Hobbs, Tempo, Main and now Im on Valley Circle walking around 'The Square' I know exactly where I am, and where I have been, and I am 'aware' of my surroundings, the people the shops the cafes the bistros the trattorias the coffee shops the restaurants the delis, I am perfectly 'aware', soon I/ll turn on Garden and see where I/ll end up, can always eat later, fewer people here, seems like Ive been walking a long time but doesnt feel like it, quieter here too fewer cars traffic sounds so far away, trees probably block the sound dull it, part of the campus I always liked, wouldnt think its a major university more like a suburban campus, trees and bushes even some paths, cant see the parking structure, just over that hill from here, cant see the street either, such a small decline blocks everything out, just the trees and shrubs and bushes and whatever, sit for a few minutes oh wow that feels good, god bless whoever thought to put a bench here, must have been walking fast, feels like anyway, actually its a bit of a distance, couple of miles I guess, or more…can really feel it in my legs now that Im sitting, and my back…can feel my breathing slowing down too, must have been really pushing it…yeah, nothing like a little aerobics for strength and health. Really pretty place. Even a slight breeze down here. Faint but noticeable. Especially on my face, must have been sweating. The air is so sweet, no perfume of flowers, just sweet clean, I guess thats what it is it smells clean and sweet and feels so refreshing I could sit here all night, yeah, does feel like its getting late but the suns still up, can see it bouncing off the leaves in the top of the trees. Really pretty. Sparkles. Glitters, thats it, glitters. Probably be a pretty sunset tonight. Wonder what kind of food I want? Suddenly feel ravenous. Must have walked up an appetite. Didnt realize it until I sat down in this idyllic little spot. Like the world doesnt exist. Keep getting hungrier and hungrier. What do I want to eat? Just hungry. Maybe I/ll just stop in the first place I come to. See how it feels. May just as well cut through the campus. Pleasant. Cool. Walk slowly and enjoy the scenery—Yeah, maybe Barnards feeling feverish. Cant eat. His wife will ask him whats wrong and he/ll tell her its his stomach, must have been something he ate. Must be tainted tunafish. Now that sounds good, very good, Tainted Tunafish. Repeat after me class, Tainted Tunafish. Tainted Tunafish. *Very* good. Now once again, Tainted Tunafish. Tainted TUNafish. And what do we get from Tainted Tunafish? Altogether now…S I C K. He should make Ripleys Believe It Or Not, ordered a salad and a coke, and got sick from Tainted Tunafish….

The man moves merrily, happily through the trees, along paths and walkways, trees and bushes casting long shadows in the evening sun. Such a joyful buoyancy to his step, such an expansiveness to his demeanor as he treads across the grass, stopping frequently to enjoy the flowers, breathing deeply of this salutary atmosphere, not noticing as he steps from grass to concrete, totally immersed and involved in his thinking and the joyous sensations it creates in his body, the lightness of foot and shoulders, flowing through the lengthening shadows, feeling them brush his cheek and finds himself sitting at a sidewalk table and ordering one of the specials with a slight wave of his hand, a broad smile and jaunty and jovial attitude, then leaning back in his chair and sipping his aperitif as his shadow stretches itself, leisurely, across the pavement.

Dont know how long it takes for E.coli to start working, I mean when he would feel it. Information doesnt apply to this situation. Possible may only get slight upset. Well, that doesnt have to be a disaster...Actually might be fine...could work out very well...yeah...yeah, we could have lunch together every few weeks or so. Oh yeah, that could be even better. If he just gets slightly sick the doctor wouldnt even think of checking for E.coli...well maybe. Good chance give him some maalox or something. Eventually might check, but for a while it would just be an 'undiagnosed chronic condition'. Oh that would be great: What in the hells wrong with me doc, I cant stand this much longer, been going on for months. Having a hard time working, falling behind and Im up for review in a couple of months. And my wifes complaining. I cant be late in getting my reports to Washington I cant tell you what its like to get that bureaucracy on your back, you cant explain anything to them even if you can find someone to explain the situation to, its like trying to nail jello to the wall and I—

Whoa, slow down there. Youll only make it worse. It may take time but—

But thats exactly what Ive been trying to tell you, I dont have—

Please, Mr Barnard, you must try and relax—squeezing his shoulders slightly and smiling—you have been under a great deal of stress and it is definitely aggravating the situation.

Mr Barnard sighed and leaned back against the examining table and nodded his head, Okay...yeah...I guess youre right—shaking his head as he stared at the floor, then raised his head slowly and looked at the doctor with such intense sadness and pleading he was happy his patient had medical insurance or he might be tempted, or at least hard pressed, to bill him personally (*heehee*)

Heres the name of a doctor I want you to see, an allergist.

Allergist? I dont understand—shaking his head, his face twisted with confusion—the problems in my stomach so—

Allergies are devious devils. An allergy, or allergies, can actually produce the symptoms you are complaining about and I feel it would be more effective to investigate the possibility of your problem being due to allergies before we undertake the many faceted and lengthy gastro-intestinal tests. Much more comfortable too—smiling in his best reassuring manner—And if it is an allergy your condition may be corrected with a simple pill—patting Mr Barnard on the back and smiling reassuringly—In the meantime relax and take it easy and call Dr Jansen as soon as you get back to your office. Okay? —tapping him on the shoulder.

The hangdog look clung to Barnard tenaciously, eating its way, like leprosy, under his skin, through his muscles and tendons, seeking out pathways to eat its way through his body, into his bones and their very marrow, into his blood and slowly eat away his brain; and too, like a cancer starting in the innermost parts of his body, ravenous cells chewing and clawing their way through bone and muscle, tissue and tendon, biting, ripping, devouring but not killing, but rather savoring the delicious process of painful and agonizing destruction.

There was no joy in Barnardville again that night as party pooper daddy dragged his depressed self through the front door, his *sotto voce* greeting being absorbed by the rug as the children ignored him and his wife grunted and mumbled, Its home.

Dessert, sir?

Huh???? Oh no, no. Thank you. Just the check.

What a heart warming smile on the mans face. It would gladden the heart of one and all who might look upon it. The man deserves to feel self-satisfied as he stands, stretches just a mite, turns his neck, rolls his shoulders, and ambles his way toward home.

It might be many, many months before he finds out what is wrong with him, a slow and continuous degeneration. Or he might slowly recover and we can have lunch again. A slow succumbing to a chronic illness. How beautiful.

But you promised, Daddy, you promised.

Im sorry sweetheart, but I dont feel well. I have to rest this weekend. Some other time.

But you said that last weekend.

The man looks at his wife with pleading eyes asking for her to intercede on his behalf, and she looks at him with confusion and concern.

What is it, Harry? Youre suddenly so distant. You never

want to be with us. You—

Thats not true, Belinda. I just dont feel well and I—

I dont know, Harry, it seems strange to me that you suddenly are so sick you cant be with your family and you have never had a sick day in your life—on the verge of tears, trembling slightly, hugging herself.

But, Belinda—reaching for her, she jerking away—

No, Harry, please dont touch me. I dont know what youre doing to be so 'tired' but I know its not from spending time with us.

I told you over and over I have to stay late at the office because Im just not getting my work done, I have no choice.

Well, obviously your choice is *not* to be with your family la—

(ah yes, the children. Two little girls…lets see…yes, about 5 and 6 and as cute as buttons or pins or whatever little girls are as cute as)

The two little girls back away, their heads and eyes downcast, their little girl worlds crumbling one little brick at a time, cracks and fissures in the mortar, bits of stone being chipped away, tears rolling silently from their suffering eyes, little girl arms and cheeks twitching, clinging to each other for safety for surely the Heavens and God Himself will hurl a lightening bolt of punishment for being so bad that mummy and daddy are fighting, clinging ever so desperately, backing away more and more, hoping they can escape the wrath of Heaven and God Almighty but what can they do as they watch dear mummy and daddy engaged in mortal combat and where will it all end…

...thats all it is, Belinda, theres no great mystery. I just am exhausted.

Not too exhausted to 'work' all the time.

Oh, how many times do I have to tell you, its because it takes me so long to do a simple job. I cant tell y—

Obviously! Comeon girls, get your things together.

Okay, Mummy.

The little cutie pies put their backpacks on and start walking toward the door, walking in a wide arc around their dear daddy. Dear daddy watches as his wife shoots him a last despairing look before leaving the house and starting on the trip to Disneyland.

Do you feel left out in the cold Barnard? You feeling disenfranchised? You feeling tortured and tormented by the very system you help perpetuate? That efficient monstrosity of attrition calculated on the fact that if people are continually turned down eventually they lack the energy to continue to try and get what is rightfully theirs, rights that were established by the Congress of the United States and aborted by slime-balls like you. How much longer will you have the energy to show up at your office and take your place in the building of brick walls erected to destroy people like me? Perhaps soon that very system will eliminate you because you have expended your energy. Oh how ironic, how poetic. Struggle Barnard. Struggle to get out of bed in the morning, struggle to shower, to shave, to somehow get into your clothes and then hope you have enough time for a cup of coffee to help you drive to work and take your place in the system of assassins. Perhaps youll hang on your own petard. Perhaps you will watch your devoted wife and cute little girls walk out of the house never to return. Think of the frantic phone calls youll make to her family, the pleading for just one word. Think. Theyre on their way to Disneyland and a fun filled day of squeals and laughter while you struggle to get work done, work that should have been all wrapped up last week but here it is, on your desk at home waiting for you…waiting for you Barnard. Better get in there before the opportunity to deny another veteran his rightful benefits fritters away.

The man is so moved by the plight of Mr Barnard that he is as yet unaware that he is home, jacket hung in the closet, tie off, collar unbuttoned, stretched out in his chair with a remote in his hand. Is the television on? He doesn't know. It is of no importance for nothing can intrude itself upon his consciousness at the moment. The remote seems to keep him in balance, to help him concentrate on his thoughts, for as long as it is solidly in his hand he searches for nothing outside himself.

…wait…suppose he does die? What then? All his agony will be over. Oh no! He cant die. He must stay alive, he absolutely must. He has to pay for all the pain and misery hes caused. He cant get off scot free like that. He must stay alive. Its only just. There has to be at least a semblance of justice somewhere in this world. People like Barnard cant keep getting off the hook like that. Why should they always go free and the rest of us pay with our blood for their crimes? Yeah, we pay, but only after a lifetime of suffering. The VA is supposed to be there to help us but instead they devise this system to frustrate us so we/ll stop trying to get the benefits we deserve, and guys like Barnard happily keep the system going, getting higher ratings and salaries for every one of us they force to discontinue appealing, time after time, board after board, over and over god how can they be so cruel its like the mafia and the teamsters, I have to pay more for the food I eat just because they dont mind killing people, yeah, thats it, you dont give them their graft they simply kill you, just like that, and what are you going to do about it? What can you do about it? Cant fight City Hall. But maybe you can burn it down. And maybe Barnard is just the beginning of it and he/ll just keep burning without dying, oh god, dont let him die, please let him live a long, long life, please, dont let him off the hook so easily—hey wait…yeah…it might be even better. His soul might suffer eternal agony. Maybe the fires of hell are real with cool, refreshing water always just out of reach, torturing him just as he has tortured so many thousands of us. His family would suffer at first, but they/d get over it yeah, yeah, his wife would remarry in a couple of months and she and the kids will forget he ever existed oh how beautiful, how exquisitely frustrating, he wouldnt even be able to haunt her, he couldnt pull any of that spooky spook stuff because she doesnt even know he exists and anyway, he wouldnt know how to haunt her, his specialty is haunting veterans, driving us to the grave well it looks like hes met his match, this is one appeal hes not going to be able to lie his way out of, his sleaze-ball weaseling isnt going to do him any good while hes chewing dirt and hosting worms. I wonder if I should go to the funeral. Pay my last respects. Yeah, sure, listen to some punk eulogize him. No thanks. Oh no, the bad will not be interred with his bones. I/ll see to that. Yes, that would be wonderful. Get a list of every veteran he tortured and send them a copy of the death notice. Be an expensive proposition. All those thousands of copies, envelopes, stamps. Yes, of course, it would be foolish and foolhardy. Im not serious. But still, isnt it pretty to think about? Oh, look at that, it must be the end of the 11oclock news. Should be getting feverish by now. Throw up in the middle of the night. Many times. Retch so much feels like a hernia. His wife all upset, she should call an ambulance, the doctor, 911, take him to the hospital, bathe his head…

Ah, there, the television has been turned off and he walks with a light tread to the bedroom, undresses, dispensing with his clothing carefully before taking a hot shower. When he stretches out on the bed he is suddenly and overwhelmingly aware that his body is exhausted as it seems to fold into itself and almost dissolve.

Maybe I should call him to see how he is no thats insane…

He turns on his side and is quickly asleep, asleep as noiselessly and dreamlessly as only the innocent experience. In the morning he slowly and comfortably leaves sleep behind him and lies on his back, listening to the song of mockingbirds, smiling, before sitting up and going to the bathroom. There is no urgency in his mind or body. The very air he moves through is light and gentle, caressing and soothing his body, greeting him with the promise of another day of fulfillment.

...true, I could call now...but theres no rush. Its as it is whether I call now or wait a few more minutes. Hmmm, it is a nice morning. Maybe a walk around the block. Why not.

Oh yeah, it is pleasant. Birds sure are enjoying it. All over the lawns. Wow isnt that something. Robins the only ones I see do that. Hop around and suddenly bam, they shove their beaks into the ground and tug out a worm. Wonder how they do that? Can they really see it? Bam! just like that. Other birds just peck at the ground, seeds and stuff I guess. Cant be the only ones eat worms. Early bird and all that. Maybe worms are scarce thats why there arent more worm eaters. Lots of bird noises this morning. Mockingbirds are the beauties though. Hey look out! You stupid squirrel, you almost got killed. Driver didnt even see him. Almost ran right under the car. Youd better stay in that tree buddy. Not safe down here. That jay sure was on his tail. Must have been too close to the nest. Dont mess with the jays there squirrel. Theyre killers. Peck you to death. Nature certainly is strange. Beautiful morning, birds singing, and all kinds of mayhem going on. Not safe to be a small creature around here. Rose bushes are pretty though. Trees too. Hang in for hundreds of years sometimes. They get zapped too. All go sooner or later. Even me. Wonder when that will be? Is that true, such a short time ago I was hoping to go now???? How could I have felt so overwhelmed by...by...whatever I felt so overwhelmed by? Just life. Nothing in particular. No tragic trauma. Just life. No purpose. No reason to bother getting out of bed, go through another day. I felt so dead. Hard—impossible to imagine on a morning like this. Life is sweet, precious, to be savored, nurtured, lived. Thats right, lived. Lets hear it class, Life is for liv—what a difference. Air smells good. Even the traffic has a comfortable sound to it. Fresh cut grass. Good pickings there. Sprinklers in the sun. So pretty. Mist floats. Little puddles for the birds. Really cool. The water. Ahhhh... No need to call now. Plenty of time. No need to know the time. Get some work done when I get home. I can call whenever I choose. Its all up to me...

All play and no work can make Jack broke. All these years working with computers and never knew the other info on the Internet. Sure I heard, but...anyway its all there. Anonymous. No name change to protect the innocent. No vocal idiosyncrasy to be remembered. No cops and robbers, 007 or Austin Powers. Oh I love you sweet baby. The love of my life. Youre so good to me. You should have been with me this morning. You would have loved it. Beautiful sky. Not too hot, cool enough for you. Trees and bushes blooming. Lots of flowers. Birds, birds, birds. Maybe you heard them. Never stopped. So many lovely colors. Oh yeah, even a dumb squirrel. Damn near ran right under the wheels of a car. Can you believe it? A jay was on his back, screeching and squawking. He was really mad. Must have gotten too close to his nest. Poor squirrel didnt know which was worse, the car or the jay. I/ll give you a treat when I finish this project. Put on *Louvre* CD and let you browse for a while. It wont take me too much longer...

Good to stretch. Productive morning. Yeah, very good. Wonder what time it is—oh no, not going to get me looking at the clock. Not playing that game. I/ll call when I decide to call. Find out then what happened. Maybe. Hell, he couldve dropped dead on his way to work and they might not know. Well, anyway, no guarantee his office knows anything. Yeah, that sure as hell is true, dont know anything about anything. Like a bunch of crazy Russians, *Nyet*. Thats all those bastards know, *Nyet*. What time is it? *Nyet*. Where is the restroom? *Nyet*. Thats a nice tie youve got on. *Nyet*. Thats all they know. From DC to all the states: *Nyet*, *Nyet*, *Nyet*. Wouldnt give you the time of day. Its madness. No, its not. Madness is uncontrollable. This is deliberate, created and perpetuated to frustrate and maim. No cop-out of madness. No relinquishing of responsibility. Its not that they created a monster, they *are* the monster. Every second of pain, every dream shattered, every life destroyed all a result of their planning. They did it. Still doing it. How can they live with themselves? How can their families? What kind of kids will they raise? Mass murderers? Or kids who just pull the wings off flies? I dont understand this world. So many rotten, evil people with so much control. How does it happen? Why does it happen? How many people have even heard the name Barnard? Its not like Eichmann. Yet whats the difference? Just as evil. Its all so rotten, rotten to the core. Only people like me know his name. And curse it. People who have been cheated, savaged and hounded by this vile inexcusable vermin. How many have been pushed over the edge by his cruelty, spending their lives in some back ward of the VA Psychiatric Hospital, spittle dribbling from their mouths, condemned to live forever in the horror Barnard created, their fragile minds surviving the horrors of war, but unable to accept that the government they defended would not only turn its back on them but tantalize them with lies that breed false hope, which is in reality a system of torture with Barnard the willing perpetrator and perpetuator, how many have already given up and simply laid down and died or struggled to feed themselves and their families, hoping that some day they will be granted what they should already have but they too were eventually destroyed oh you are a rotten son of a bitch, how can anyone treat another human being like this, they did nothing to you yet you delight in torturing them oh I hope there is a hell so you can roast in it oh shit, that rotten bastard, been feeling great and he poisons me we/ll see whats going on.

Mr Barnards office.

Ah… I/d like to speak to Mr Barnard.

Hes out to lunch, can I take a message?

No… no, thats alright. I/ll try again later.

Hes at work… Out to lunch… Cant be too sick…

Hmm... May not even be sick... Wonder...

Maybe hes not really eating. Could be. Might be sitting in the sun or lying down in the lounge. Yeah. Not eating at all. Maybe hes in the bathroom. Sure. Could be. Wouldnt tell his secretary Im going to spend an hour in the bathroom. Like I said yesterday, best thing might be if hes still alive. This might be the answer to a prayer. Yes. Yes. Oh boy, I know it is. Its all coming together. I can feel it in my bones. Yes. Yes. Yes. Thank you god. It will all come together. Its all in the process. Right now. Yes. Damn, Im starving. Maybe Barnard cant eat, but I can. Haha, I wish I could pass some pickled herring under his nose. Oh, you know what would be great??? oysters. Some nice, gray, slimy oysters. Jiggle them in their shells. Oh god, a real winner, haha, put the oysters on a calfs brain, a nice bowl of brains all wiggling around with oysters, yech, makes me want to puke. Forget about that. Guess should keep it simple and just fry some eels and watch them wiggle in the pan. Yeah, nice and simple. Oh, sometimes I think Im awful. Follow all this with a hot fudge sundae. Oh sir, you are too cruel. Could be. But its not going to stop me from eating. Decisions, decisions. Fix something here or go out? Kinda restless. Walk to the deli would be good. Unwind. Still not too hot. Yeah. Good idea. Stroke of genius. Well, up and atem.

And so it has come to pass that he has shaken off the disappointment and depression and is once again one with the sunshine and light. Can such a man do aught but prevail? Is he not destined to be victorious in all his endeavors?

Hot pastrami or brisket? Decisions, decisions. What am

I in the mood for? Whatever. Food here is fresh. Cant be too careful these days. Lot of salmonella and E.coli around. Think I/ll go for the cheese and avocado. Yeah. Sounds good. An ice tea and I am ready for whatever the day has to offer. Yes. Bring on the day. No. Not interested in giants. Hmmm, yeah, maybe clowns. Yeah, they may be in order. Just what the doctor ordered, to coin a phrase. Just the day and whatever comes along with it. I/ll see. Maybe later. If the mood strikes me. It is up to me. Perhaps not in its entirety, not the whole megillah, so to speak, but the actions are of my domain. Results…well, dependent on many factors, basic health, strength of immune system, stress, oh yeah, stress, but certainly not conscience. No problem for Barnard…any of them, those…ah th—no. Emphatically. Not going to aggravate myself because of their inhumanity. Going to enjoy my lunch, the day, the birds, the bees, whatever, and if I am in the mood to call this afternoon I will simply pick up the phone, dial the number and see how our friend is faring. Its all up to me. Right now I am going to slowly eat this sandwich and watch that red-headed waitress. An absolute stroke of genius. Wonder who first thought of it. Brilliant. Mini-skirts on waitresses. Every time they bend over a table theres the thought of heaven. Dont really see that much, actually less than a pair of shorts. The hint. Expectancy. If she bends just the tiniest bit more. Delicious. Absolutely delicious. Yeah, the sandwich too. But this is more than the food of life. We are talking nitty gritty here. There are some things more important than food. Unless youre starving of course. But there are other things that create greater hunger than the thought of food. When youre satisfied.

Actually a pretty good sandwich. Should really go there more often. Keep forgetting how much I like it. Great ice tea too. Best in town. Dinners pretty good too. Maybe go back tomorrow no, I dont have to look at the clock or not look at the clock. *I* certainly am not making a big thing out of this. Its just not important what the time is. I/ll call or I wont call. Its up to *me*. A little more work first, then do whatever I do.

...yeah, well, it is difficult. Didnt expect this much trouble. Tacky problem, but still... Maybe this way...

Thats enough for today. Not a bad day. Pretty much up to date. O-o-o krist, it feels good to stretch...

Mr Barnard, please.

Im sorry, he had to leave early today.

Oh... Will he be in tomorrow morning?

He said he would. But to tell you the truth, he didnt look so good so Im not sure.

Oh...I see.

Can I take a message?

No, thats alright. Thanks.

Yes thanks...thanks, thanks, 'thanks a million, a million thanks to you'... What sweet music to my ears. Didnt look so good. Wonder how bad he looked? Diarrhea? Might be messy by the time he gets home.

Oh yes! Yes! Lets hope so. Dont blame it on the poor dog. Of course he has a dog. They always have a dog. Bet Barnard does too... Hi big fella, how you doin, heh, heh, oh let me scratch this belly... Yeah, let *me* scratch *your* belly, the belly of the beast you son of a bitch. If anyone treated your dog the way you treat us youd killem, right on the spot killem dead. Yeah, thats the way those monsters are, love their dogs and despise people. Go out of their way to make our lives miserable and impossible, but their dogs, oh they get the best of everything. How many people would love to be treated that well? Millions! Millions just in this country alone, and the whole world? God theyre sick...evil, millions of kids in this country go to bed hungry, if they even have a bed, and what he spends on his dog would feed those kids for a month, ahh, whats the use, just drop it, screwim...wonder if I should have asked that guy what was wrong, I mean how he was sick? He might have thought it funny if I did. Yeah. Couldnt askim if he had diarrhea or if he spent his lunch hour in the restroom sitting on the throne even if Barnard is a royal pain in the ass.

Feels like another nice day. Hmmm, wonder if its the same mockingbird? What do they like to eat? Pet store. Maybe get to one later. Finches are nice too. See if they eat the same food. Well...up and atem.

Nothing like a hot shower. What an invention. One of the finest gifts of civilization. Hot shower, cold rinse. In summer anyway. Sometimes winter. Brisk rub with towel. Ready to go. Great thing about summer is air drying. Ohh, thats great. Tarzan air dried. Waterfall for shower, lakes and rivers for a tub. Look out for those crocagators. They will definitely alter your anatomy. Haha, I like that one, alter your anatomy. Chew you into little pieces. Always someone on the top of the waterfall, spying and scheming. Some of those Bwanas were almost as bad as Barnard. The natives knew better than to screw around with Tarzan. He was one bad dude. Lions, rhinos, just him and his knife. Great penthouse and elevator. Wouldnt last long in Brooklyn. Busted for indecent exposure. Me Tarzan, you Judge. That is absolutely correct, and you are going to do sixty days. Try dressing as Beau Brummel the next time. Next case! Hey, he was the first hippie. Peace and Love Tarz. No, not now. Call later. Plenty of time. Thats right. Absolutely right. Its all up to me. Call him now or later. Pirate Jenny knew. From mockingbirds to showers, to Tarzan, to Pirate Jenny. Perfect sense. Beautiful day and all makes sense. Haha, even the senseless. Thank god no ones listening. Im listening to my stomach. Been a while since Ive had breakfast at the deli. Yeah. Get a paper. Relax. Of course I can look at the phone. Not going to spend the rest of the day standing here staring at it. When I want to.

Oh, feel that air. Even smells good. Mustve been smoking Tarzans banana skins. It does smell good though. Maybe the birds were eating the same skins. They like the air. Singing their asses off. Air feels good on my skin. Walking makes you aware of being alive. Legs move, feet go up and down...and forward, heartbeats, lungs breathe in air...and exhaust fumes, and smog, and other forms of pollution. Keeps us alive. Bodies need poison. Withdrawals without it. Toxin-free airs a killer. Trade places with a Hunza and we/d both drop dead. Can deal with this. This air, no pollution, crystal clean water, apricot pits. No thanks. Not even a bagel with lox and cream cheese. Thats not living. Pizza. Egg rolls. Cafe latte. I prefer civilization. I am a civilized man. Product of. Member of. Endorser of. Proponent of. Proselytizer for. The simple and ecstatic pleasure of civilization. Like so: I feel the air and sunshine around me, feel the warmth of my blood from walking, push open the doors and feel the cool air, smell the food, uuummmmm, hear the clatter and chatter, see and feel the hustle and bustle. Ahh, civilization, I embrace you.

One?

Yes, just one.

You ready to order?

Yes. A couple of eggs, hash browns, seeded roll, and a cafe latte.

How do you want your eggs?

Bright eyed and bushy tailed, looking me right in the eye... You have a beautiful smile.

Thank you. Want any juice or fruit?

No. No thanks.

Coffee right away?

Yes, please.

Coming right up.

Same old headlines. Ah, there is good news, the Dodgers lost again. Three in a row, 5 out of 7. I knew I was supposed to buy a paper today. Oh great, they blew a 2 run lead in the ninth. This guy sounds surprised. Now thats amazing. Thought I felt as good as I could this morning, yet I feel even better now. Does that mean theres no limit to how good you can feel? I guess. Within limits. Maybe you just feel better and better until you explode? Never heard of it. Always something kicks in. Then down the tubes. Never feel too good. Maybe thats craziness. Feel so good your mind explodes. Cant handle it. How come you can feel worse and worse? No matter how bad you feel you can always feel worse. A rotten arrangement. Sometimes you can assert yourself. Yeah. And bounce up. You see the problem and know what to do. Its like life is right with you. Feel bad and everything goes wrong until you lose your mind. Feel good and everything goes right BUT you dont have to lose your mind. You dont have to let life drag you down, again. Yeah, thats it. People bounce back and forth, up and down, feel good, feel bad, because they have not really identified the problem in their lives, they are the puppets of life rather than the masters of their own existence. Thats where they make their mistake. They let life push them up until theres no place to go but down, kaflosh. The Black Hole of Calcutta. The Pits. No equilibrium. Avoid extremes. Excess is the problem. Balance the answer. Yes. Oh, by all means, Yes! Take all necessary steps to eliminate the problem. No matter what its form. Animal, vegetable or mineral. Life is made up of zillions of individuals. Some create an excessive imbalance. Most of us a little this way a little that way…hey, it all evens out. Not with everyone. Some far exceed all acceptable limits. Thats the problem. Yes. Yes indeed. Must be corrected. There are a few whose destiny it is to help bring about that balance. Those who have been ordained to be a part of the answer and help eliminate those who are so severely 'out of balance'. Like a surgeon. If an infected limb threatens the life of the entire being, then the limb must be amputated. All agree. Life must go on at all costs. Life will always see to that. No one applies for the job. Life appoints them. Perhaps not all accept. Who knows how many? Cant tell. I have accepted. Fully. Totally. I will fulfill my commitment to life.

The man has become aware that he has been appointed to pursue a mission, one that he has already embarked upon with dispatch and great enjoyment. That is the fact that we need to concentrate on. Look at the expression of his shoulders as he walks home, slapping the folded paper against his leg. What remarkable energy, and lack of swagger. The very nature of his walk indicates a great humility. He enters his house and tosses the paper on the couch, looks at the phone for a moment, then shakes his head.

Later. Much too early. There, or not there, doesnt prove anything. Just have to call again later. Bad idea. Same voice on the other end. Will recognize the same voice calling over and over. Nothing suspicious. Nothing out of the ordinary. Must stay in tune with the higher order that is guiding me. Now Im not sure what I thought before. Justified? Yes. By all means. Yes. Emphatically. Knew it was necessary. Desperately needed. How else to balance the evil committed by one man to so many? Absolutely: Justified! Necessary! No qualms. No guilt. Do what is needed. But now???? Dont know. Somethings changed. Dont really know what...or how... Not really. Feel different...somehow. But feels good. Enough for now. Yeah, too soon to know whats really happening. But somethings gnawing at me. Like something on the tip of your tongue. Like something wants me to know. Is trying to tell me. I can smell it. Taste it. Feel lighter somehow. Weird. Dont feel like Ive lost anything. Actually...yeah, feels like somethings added. Oh, oh, oh. Seems crazy— No, it doesnt. Feels sane. How can that be? How can I feel sane? Never thought like that before. Sane. What does that mean? Feels so right though. I feel sane. Like really simple. Nothing exciting...or...or weird like. Just sane. Scary. Arent you nuts if you feel sane? Sane. Never thought of this before. Doesnt make sense now that I think about it. How can feeling sane mean youre crazy? Okay, okay. Enough of this goofiness. If ev—Webster. Yeah. He/ll know. Lets see...okay, here we go...sand-worm, sand-wort, sandy...sandy, consisting of, containing, or sprinkled with sand. Well now, who would have thought. Thats interesting. So, sane, free from disease: HEALTHY, mentally sound, able to anticipate and appraise the effect of one's actions. Not a word about being nuts if you feel sane. Still not sure why that word came to mind. Seems like I felt something was missing. Like what??? lets see...whats missing, whats...of course, not hysterical. Yeah! Sane. No hysteria. I certainly can anticipate and appraise the effect of my actions. Yeah, youre damn right I can. Absolutely. No hysteria. So…haha, this is so funny. Goofy. Spending all this time wondering about feeling sane. Sure felt nuts enough. I/ll take this. No hysteria. Absolutely. Must remain anonymous. Utmost importance. No ego boost. Killer. Need to prove something. Revenge. Real trap. Let the world know what I did. Hysteria. Death. Stupid. Truly stupid. Sacrifice yourself for revenge. Starting to make sense. Yeah. Okay… Yeah…does seem easier. Almost like its out of my hands. Hmmm… Strange. All strange. But feels so right. Yeah… Yeah, leave it alone. Just let it come. Pushing leads to hysteria. It/ll come. Strong sense, I/ll see when I need to see. Good time to get to work. Yeah, my sweetheart, time to turn you on. Yes, yes, yes, a little work and then, perhaps, a phone call. When Im ready.

Ohh, must have been at this a long time, shoulders and neck stiff. Arg, cant rotate them…a little anyway…ohh, thats better. Decompression time. Seems like the machine sucks me right into it sometimes. Like Ive been on a trip. Little disoriented. Yeah, right. Decompression. Dont pop to the surface too soon. Ahh, that feels better. Stretch this, stretch that. Youd think I was an athlete instead of a computer engineer. Maybe chess. Some of those guys run. Prefer walking. In a hurry, drive. Wow, look at the time. Was in there quite a while.

Mr Barnard please.

Mr Barnard isnt in.

Oh… Will he be back soon?

Afraid not. Can I help you with something?

Nooo, afraid not. Really need to speak to him. When is he expected back?

We have no idea. Hes in the hospital.

Hospital? (no, no, no singing, no hallelujahs) Whats wrong with him?

Not sure. Food poisoning maybe.

Sorry (jesus, no laughing) to hear that.

Can I take a message? Maybe someone else can help you.

No, no thanks.

It may be a while before he gets back.

It can keep.

Oh yes, oh yes, it can keep… And keep and keep and keep. Oh, I should have asked him how he got food poisoning. Probably that nasty coffee shop. Board of Health should shut that place down. Maybe he/ll sue them. Or his heirs. Heirs and assigns, heirs and assigns. What a day, what a day. 'Oh what a beautiful morning', morning, afternoon whats the difference, the Dodgers lost again and Barnards in the hospital Oh happy days are here again. Whoa, better quiet down a bit, the neighbors might wonder what all the noise is about. Too early for a party, might think someone is killing me. Im killing me. This is so wonderful…beyond belief, so far beyond belief. I was hoping…trying not to hope but hoping, thinking, thinking, but this is beyond all expectations. I cant ever recall feeling so happy, so elated, so…so solid…so excited…yeah, how incredible…so excited and peaceful. All that work, the research, preparations, administration, the incredible fear and it worked. It all worked. I feel so...so...right, so validated. Yeeaahh validated!!!! Its all coming together. Hes not dead yet, but I know what Im doing. I did it. The culture worked. It worked. I can duplicate it anytime I want. Maybe he *is* dead by now. Feel like Zorba the Greek dancing, spinning, thats me Zorba... Yes... Val-I-dAted. The gods are smiling and shining. Validate. Vali—no, wait...wait...yeah... Oh yeah, Im not just validated, Im sanctioned. YEAH YEAH YEAH SANCTIONED!!!! Whoa, better plop on the couch and sit for a while, getting dizzy spinning around in circles. Enough of Zorba. Everythings enough. I AM SANCTIONED! Yes! Of course, thats what I was feeling, thats what was on the tip of my tongue, the thing I could taste. Ohh, better start calming down. No hysteria. Sane. Oh how blessed. Indeed. Sanctioned. Okay, okay, let it go...breathe in...breathe out...breathe in...breathe out... Thats it. Slow down. S l o w d o w n... Good. Oh, the paper. Never did read the comics. Thats it. Easy. Just breathe in and out. Yeah... Deserve celebration. Wind down. Paper helps. Meaningless prattle. Page after page. What the hell. Haha, thats really funny. Im reading the obits. Didnt know it. How wonderful. Couldnt write something like that. Whod believe it. Too corny. Never did it. Say first sign of age. Obits. Guess they like to think they won. Still here reading others obits. Yeah. Well I cant wait. Could call the hospital. Later. Dont know theyll tell me hes dead. I guess theyll give him a big spread. He was rotten enough to be praised. Nice black border around it. Maybe in color. Magenta border. Blue type. Oh yeah, flowers and butterflies around the edges. Slugs and leeches would be more appropriate. No, we wont speak ill of the dead. Why bother? Just knowing hes dead is enough. Cold stone dead. So who did die? Hmmm, not one familiar name. All survived by a 'loving' somebody. Husband, wife, children, dogs, cats, bill collectors... Amazing how many people love each other in the obits. Easier there than anywhere else. Survived by a dog. Who paid for the obit? ASPCA. With love, Fido. His dog will missim. Hope his wife—widow—celebrates. Not even get a headstone. Dropim in a hole. Yeah...every spouse loves every deceased. You bet. But when they were alive? I can see them looking down on him, laid out in a casket, and saying I love you. Oh yeah. I love you. You make my heart go pitter patter, patter patter, kaflunk. How about a James Earl Jones deep resonant I love you? Works for me. Immolations nuts. Some women jump in his grave. True to the end. What a tradition...sentence. Your husbands dead so burn bitch. Worlds nuts. Control their wives even when dead. Yeah, death can perpetuate tyranny. Create martyrs. Cleanse tyrants. Death is no equalizer. Can be a magnifier. Lot invested in death. Belief systems. After life. Hocus pocus. Let us now extol the virtues of this fine and noble man, who gave so generously and unstintingly of himself to make life easier for others. Who, who...where, where???? Wonder what you feel? Doesnt seem so inviting now. Livings better. Do you hear people crying??? laughing??? the dirt on the box? Too spooky.

Deads dead. Well no, hes not dead…yet. Soon. No hurry. Does a coma hurt? Seems painless. Wonder. No, no need to wish that. The act is just, as is the result. Enough. Life goes on. What follows may also be just. His replacement may be just. Possible. No longer has anything to do with me. Im free of him and the torment. May not give me any info. Can call anyway, but… Wonder what makes a man be like that? Cause so much trouble for people. Guess he just doesnt care. Does he know now? Will he ever be aware? Find out when dead? No point. Well, yeah, if reincarnations real. Hows it work, come back as a leper? Gone. No bells. Come back as an ice cream truck. Yeah…a dingaling. Oh well, Im allowed. Really starting to feel restless. Could walk around the square. Browse. Not tempting. Suddenly sluggish. Lethargic. What the hell???? Ass dragging. Need to eat. Thatll help. Dont really feel like eating. Hungry though. Idea of fixing something or going to a restaurant seems impossible. Like I/d rather starve than bother. Damn. This is nuts. Eyes so heavy. Why in the hell should I be tired? Plenty of energy just a minute ago. Yeah…I guess…but feel too tired to call. In a minute maybe. Dont care. Like, not important. Damn! feeling so great and wham, cant get off the couch. Weighed down. Legs weigh a ton. Jesus, like when I wanted to shoot myself. Well, big difference. But body feels almost the same. No reason to feel so sad. Out of nowhere. Again, wink of an eye. But not depressed. Not truly. Just sluggish. Guess I could order a pizza. Why not? In a minute. Yeah. Better than going out. Yeah, sure, I can call…just not right now. He/ll be there in an hour or so.

No, of course not. Im not afraid to find out what is happening. Hes either dead or alive and theyll tell me or they wont. Simple. No, not afraid to call. Nothing to fear. Jesus, its no big deal. This is ridiculous. Sit here debating a stupid phone call. Really think Im hungry.

Marios pizza.

Hi. I/d like to order a medium pizza, extra garlic.

Extra garlic.

Yeah.

Thats it, no extra cheese or nothing?

No. Just garlic.

Coke, Pepsi?

No, no. Just the pizza.

Gotchya. Wheres it goin?

626 Selby Avenue.

20, 25 minutes.

Good.

Feels good already. Guess Im hungrier than I thought. Got me looking at the clock already. What the hell. Still in my hand.

Veterans Administration Hospital.

I/d like to find out how a patient is.

What is their name?

Barnard. Mr Barnard.

One moment please…

Are you a member of the family sir?

No. Just a friend.

Mr Barnard is still in Intensive Care.

Is he alright…? I mean is he…?

That is all the information I have sir. You would have

to consult with a member of the family.

Oh, I see. Fine. Thank you.

Good evening sir.

So, ICU. Thats not bad. No. Not bad at all. No information. Even better. Not critical. Not dangerous. Not stable. Not anything. Good sign. May not make it through the night. 'With a little bit of luck, with a little bit of luck, with a little bit of bloomin luck.' Call tomorrow. Maybe earlier. We/ll see. Wont worry about that. Go to the coffee shop and eavesdrop. Theyll know whats happening. Somebody in his department will know. No secrets there. Wow! Yeah! Maybe the coffee shops closed. Possible. Food poisoning. Could go see. Better not eat there. If he got food poisoning there. Better safe th—Ahh, the pizza.

Well…another day, another dollar, as the saying goes. And as goes Maine so goes the Nation. Right. Right down the tubes. But not today. Ah, today. Its here. So what happens now? Now I get up and pee, then shower, then…then we/ll see what happens. So, theyre still here and still singing. Has to be a good day. Dont think I dreamt. Feel refreshed. Terrific. Finches chirp the *basso continuo*, the mockingbirds fly with the melody. Hey, thats a good one. Like that. 'Listen to the Mockingbird, Listen to the Mockingbird, and the'—I see you pussy cat trying to sneak up on that mockingbird, look out—up, there he goes, up, up and away… Better luck next time—Hey…yeah, I like that. I see you. I C U. Yeah, IC U,

IC University. Fight! Fight! Fight! Fight on for IC U. Give me an I, give me a C, give me a U. Ra, Ra, Ra!!!! The IC U… IC U what? Spartans? Trojans? Condoms? Not bad. Wildcats? Pussycats? Not macho enough. Come on, Fight, Fight, Fight for ol Pussycats? Yeah, sure. Maybe Razorbacks? Humpbacks? Hey, thats a whale of an idea. Okay, dump that too. Pelicans? Any Pelicans? I dont know. Doesnt seem to sing. Im an IC U Pelican. No pizzazz as they say. Ducks! God, how can anybody want to go to a school to be called a 'Duck'? A Spartan or Trojan, okay. Even Condom. But Duck? Fight on you Duckeepoos. Yeah, killers. Sandcrabs. Lobster backs. Cripples! Hey, thats it, The IC U Crips. Fight on oh mighty Crips, Fight on for IC U. Yeah, yeah, yeah. Fight on oh mighty Crips, Fight on for IC U. Yeah…but you dont see me. Nobody sees me. No one did see, has seen, is seeing, will see. No peekaboo, ICU. Not even a masked man who gallops toward the setting sun. Or the rising sun. Depends on the situation. If it takes all night to do in the bad guys. Anyway, he had Tonto. Him honest injun, but better nobody knows. The Shadow do, but Margo Lane???? Better not. Look what happened to Jesse James. John Dillinger. Benny One Ball. Tragic cases, one and all. Guess that pussy cat is going to have to find some mice. Didnt think of that, IC U Rats. Equal rights for rats. Good cause. Dogs. Pussy cats. Horses. Elephants. Eagles. Hairy chested nut scratcher. On and on. Every creature has someone trying to protect it. Even people. But no one cares about rats. The rat of the month club. Wont fly. That cat does alright. Here every day and hes well fed. Yeah…time to get something to eat. Another walk in the early morning light…well, not so early really. But morning. On a roll. Every time I eat there. Comes up roses. Eggs bright eyed and bushy tailed, whole wheat toast, *café au lait*, and…the paper. Yes, yes indeed. *Andiamo.*

A pleasant breakfast. Pleasant time. Really nice people. Smile a lot. Should go back tomorrow. Lots of clicking and clanging. Nice. Sort of comforting, those sounds. Smells too. Hey, the Dodgers lost again. If I eat there twice a day will they lose twice a day? Have to check it out. What the hell, one game a day is fine. Anything more might be a record. Dont want them in Guinness's for anything. Think I/ll walk around the block. Pretty good, IC U Crips. Crips with a fight song. Something wonderful about that. IC U Condoms aint bad. Nah. Crips. And nobody knows. Maybe I dont even know. Thats really safe. Nothing to feel safe from. Many have food poisoning. Happens every day. Board of Health is too lax in their inspections. Inefficiency of Government Agencies. How many deaths could be prevented each year if the government did its job? Astronomical figure. Shame. All these fast food places packed with kids. Who can make the connection? Twenty or thirty years old and they have a degenerative condition of some kind. Cant eat that poison all your life. If they cleaned up those places it would save billions in medical costs. Some one should do an exposé. Ahh, what good would it do? Lots of noise and rhetoric and in the end it is all in the hands of some bureaucrat like Barnard.

Peekaboo Barney, ICU. Feel like I could walk all day. Better get back. Get to work. Been walking quite a while. Feels good. Work beckons. I reckon. Like going home to a friend. The clicking and hum when you boot up. Best to work when ever possible. Cant predict the future. Circumstances may prevent working for a while. Possible. Anyway, if you love it do it. Hey, thats another good one. Should make a list of these goodies. Copyright them or something. Cant make a buck from everything. Some people can. It seems. Amazing the ways people can make money. Wonder if they enjoy it? Probably the challenge. Must be. Yeah...must be. Thats the thing. Money without challenge? Why bother? If you dont love it dont do it. Obvious converse. What the hell, its good too. What a wonderful thing life can be. God...wake up singing. Hot shower. Walk in pleasant weather...perfect weather. Lovely street. Pussy cat and birds in harmony. Yeah...sure. As long as the bird is swift of wing. Lose myself in work. How can people deny the existence of God? Madness. Divine order is so obvious. Could be. Divine order could be perception. I suppose its inexorable and inevitable. Oh well, all a mere bagatelle. Fight, fight, fight. Fight on for IC U, fight on to do or die. Give me a C, give me an R, give me an I, give me a P, give me a S, CRIPS, CRIPS, CRIPS. FIGHT, FIGHT FIGHT! Death before dishonor. Never daunted by the foe. We/re the Crips for ever moe. Ever onward and upward. Excelsiorrr!!!!

I look in the mans eyes, I examine his heart, and I find no fault in him. Some will disagree with much that he says, even more with what he has done, yet I see no fault in him. I judge him not. He walks, enjoys the morning, goes home and sits in front of his computer, works, and in a short time is absorbed in solving the problems and answering the questions his work presents to him this lovely morning. He will continue working until he decides to stop; he will call the hospital when he so decides. It is all up to him.

Look at that, almost three. Tempus really fugits. So…these feelings are hunger. Some day I/ll pay attention to that. Yeah, sure. Mind cant be two places at once. Guess I should eat. Too late for lunch. Could wait a couple of hours. Early dinner. What the hell. Is it healthier to have a late lunch or an early dinner? Get the search engine on it. Head still involved with work. Could watch some Bugs Bunny. Destroy half an hour finding out hes not on. Seems silly to call now. Dont know. Wait. Get latest info. Yeah, whenever I call Im getting the latest info. So, same old same old. Always tomorrow. Wow, my heads still out to lunch. Yeah, and Im hungry.

Veterans Administration Hospital, patient information.

I/d like to know how Mr Barnard is doing please.

One moment please… Im sorry sir, theres no Barnard listed.

Really? He was in the ICU (peek a boo) yesterday.

Im sorry sir. That name is not on the list of patients. Perhaps you can check with his doctor or family.

Yes… Right. Well, thank you.

Easy now. Dont get too excited. He could be alright and they sent him home… Or maybe transferred to another hospital, or she made a mistake, didnt see his name. Lot of possibilities. No point in getting excited. Calm. Could go to the coffee shop and see what I hear. Not much chance. Lunchs about all. Always tomorrow. *(Fight, fight, fight, for IC U)* Maybe go to the hospital. Do what? Comeon, anonymity. Hey, wait a second...haha, yeah...sure, the obits. Survived by his loving dog Crip, who sat at his graveside, resisting all attempts to move him, ignoring the food and water brought to him, stretched across the sod of the grave, whining, growing weaker and weaker with the passing of each day, from time to time howling at the moon then falling into sudden silence as if waiting for his beloved masters voice to reach his eager ears from the freshly dug grave, until weak from starvation and dehydration he could no longer resist the attempts to remove him and was lifted from his vigil and before he could be placed in the van 30 feet away he gave up the ghost and lay lifeless in the arms that held him. Crip was the only one to attend his funeral. It is rumored that there were celebrations in various and sundry public places including parks and community centers, as well as various veterans organizations. They all observed a moment of silence for Crip. Yeah, give me a C, give me an R, give me an I, give me a P. Yes, yes indeed, give me a P so I can piss on his grave. Whoa...take it easy. Premature. Steady. Calm down. Dont know what happened. Come on, breathe in...... Breathe out...... In...... Out...... No hysteria. Leads to mistakes. Maybe tragic. We/ll see. Okay. Thats better. Still hyped, but better. In...... Out...... Okay. No. No hospital. Not likely in paper tonight.

Remember, could be fine. Out walking with Crip. The news? Possible. Usually report food poisoning. They love that. Details. Love the details. Millions die annually. Lets see. Local station best. Four car accident? Yeah. No, no, theres another car way over there... Ohhh, look at that... Oh no, this is awful. So much violence. Disgusting. Do they really believe that that is all people are interested in? Wrecks on freeways...jaws of life...drunks running people down...cops beating people up...people shooting each other...little kids finding fathers gun and shooting friends...over and over... Cant be the only thing happening in the city. Give us a break. Must be something positive and newsworthy happening. What about the proverbial Little ol Lady in tennis shoes? What is she up to today? Feeding the pigeons in the park? Poisoning them? Shooting Pit Bulls? Thats almost as good as man bites dog. Yeah, what about mans best friend? Havent had a cross country trek to find his family in a long time. Got lost in New Hampshire and followed them all the way to Mexico City. To this day no one knows how he avoided ending up part of a taco in Tijuana. How about a dog saving a pussy cat? Or something. Cant take this on an empty stomach. Off, off. Ah, peace and quiet. No more murder and mayhem. Not here anyway. Petes. Yeah, sounds good. Im starving. Veal picatta. Linguine and clams. Dont know. Have to be careful of shellfish. Pollution. See what Im in the mood for when I get there. I suppose. But cant expect anything in tonights paper. Possible...but save it for the morning. More chance then. Save it. Makes tomorrow like Christmas. Maybe I/ll hang up my stocking. Sing carols. What the hell. Just dont wear a Santa Claus suit to breakfast. Not very anonymous. This time of year. Could always get eggplant parmigiana. Been a long time. Minestrone soup first. Sounds good. Famished.

So much work, so much extensive and intensive research, such dedication over time, never faltering, yet now, while the outcome is as yet unknown, he lives each day as if it were the last day of his life, and the first day of the rest of his life, each and every moment, every heartbeat, every breath a celebration. Yes, I cannot but admit I am in awe of the man and his commitment, and his ability to maintain such exquisite balance. Another day well lived.

The usual this morning sir? Eggs bright eyed and bushy tailed?

Its been working so far so why change now?

Working?

Im still alive.

Oh. Yes. I/ll bring your *café au lait* in a minute.

Thanks.

Well, no point in feeling around and playing games. Go right for the jugular. Ainsworth, Allen...bingo! Yeah. There it is. In black and white. Has to be true. Give me a B, give me an A, give me an R, give me an N, give me an A, give me an R, give me a D. Barnard, you sweetheart. Oh Barnard, youre a killer. Or is it killee? Oh, this is wonderful. Just wonderful. It worked. It really work—

Heres your *cafe au lait* sir. My, youre really happy this morning.

Does it show?

Oh yes. You look like youre ready to bounce around the room. Better be careful drinking your coffee.

Oh definitely.

Your stock must have gone through the roof.

Much better. Much, much better.

Wow, it must really be something to die for.

Oh yes. Yes indeedy do.

I/ll be right back with your eggs.

Okay, lets calm down now. Celebrate when we get home. Must be obvious to everyone. No. Eat your breakfast. Business as usual. No deviations. Always anonymous. Important. Dont forget. No way to link me with it. At worst food poisoning. Would never think someone responsible. No connection. Will probably check out coffee shop. Wonder what theyll think if no trace there? Suppose theyll check to see if anyone else is sick. Might think it strange hes the only one. Wonder. Could dump a little in the salad bar. Sure to get a couple then. Be no suspicion then. Conclusive. Barnard not target. Random. Yeah, especially after time lapse. Big trouble for coffee shop. Couple of people might die. Cant do that. Barnards one thing. Innocent people no. Can hardly sit still. Just finish breakfast. Usual tip. No personal connection. Even if they thought it was deliberate. He doesnt even know—knew how many people he screwed. Cant check thousands of names. Excuse me sir, my name is Horatio Q Pinkerton and I am investigating the demise of one Harry Barnard.

Harry Barnard?

Yes. He was an administrator at the Veterans Administration. Benefits division.

Demise?

Yes sir, he is dead. Totally, absolutely, and, I might add, as far as we can tell, irrevocably.

Oh.

I dont suppose you know anything about his death.

I didnt even know he was sick.

Yes…well…he was. Not anymore of course.

Of course.

Pity. Prime of life really. Great pity.

Family in turmoil?

No. Went to Disneyland I believe. Or was it Disneyworld?

Oh.

Its his dog. Crip. Broken hearted. Hasnt eaten since he went to the hospital. Ah, Harry Barnard that is, not the dog.

I see.

Thank you sir, youve been most helpful.

My pleasure… Indeed, my pleasure. Pleasure, pleasure, pleasure. Give me a P, give me an L, and all the rest of it. Really must get out of here. Lets see…yes, everythings as I usually leave it. Same tip, same place. Fine. Smile at cashier…

Have a nice day.

Thank you sir. Have a good one.

Oh that feels good to be out. Out, out. Cant go tripping the light fantastic down the street. Had no idea I would feel like this. Over powering! Feel like shouting. Its alright, I can *feel* like it. No damage. Not going to do it. Not going to tell anyone. Not that I would really consider it. Not directly. Maybe allude. Cant do that. Is that why some confess? Not conscience, just a need to talk about it with someone. Tell them how you planned it, executed, results. Powerful urge. Not confess. Just talk. There must be ways. Could go to a bar, or some such place. People always talk to strangers in bars. Wouldnt know who you are. Put on a mustache. Wear horn rimmed glasses. Comb your hair differently. Tell anyone what happened. Theyd never believe it. Yeah, sure, until they heard about it on the news. Even so, they could never connect me with Barnard. Better keep walking, wound tight. Just keep breathing. In...... Out...... Just keep breathing. Dont breathe a word. Maybe Crip. Wow, what a great idea. The only one…creature who cares. Great way to unburden your soul. Suppose he knows what Im saying? Smells me out? Man attacked by dog. Make the news. I could be on television. Dont need that. God. Its becoming unbearable. Like Im going to explode. Have to release the pressure. In…... Out…... If I could leap or jump or just spin around it might help. Try it when I get home. Pair of tights. Up and atem. Walking real fast. Necessary. No slowing down. Not now. Round and round he goes. Throat getting dry. Should have had another glass of water. Where am I???? Hmm, quite a distance from home. Mustve been almost running. Legs getting tired. Have to forget about those leaps and bounds. What the hell, stop in here for a minute. Throat really parched.

Hi. What can I do for you?

Dont know. Something wet.

Scotch & soda…extra soda?

Sounds good.

Taking a constitutional?

Yeah… I guess you could call it that.

Better do it now. Too hot in the afternoon. Here ya go. Ice cubes sound good, dont they?

Huh…oh yeah…yeah, actually they do. Ahh, cold and wet.

You dont drink much, do you?

Drink? Actually, no.

Didnt think so.

Oh?

Ive been a bartender for more than 20 years, and usually when a guy comes in a joint before 12 he doesnt look too good.

Look too good? I dont understand.

No mystery. Theyre usually hung over and have the shakes and need a hair of the dog. You just look thirsty.

Oh…oh, I see. Well, yes, I am. Took a little walk after breakfast and I guess I wandered around too long.

I do that sometimes. Start wondering about things and the next thing you know Im wherever.

Wherever…yeah, sort of. I was thinking of the book Im reading. Fascinating. About a man who needs to kill someone, and do it so it looks natural.

Oh, like the CIA, eh?

I guess. I dont know. But hes just a guy, you know?

Oh, like revenge.

Not exactly. He just needs to be eliminated. He hurts too many people.

I get it, sort of like a mercy killing.

Well, I guess maybe you could think of it like that. Yes. So anyway, he learns how to make E.coli and salmonella cultures and gets it in his coffee.

No shit? How does he do that?

At work. Pretty simple. Actually he works in a lab… in a high school. Of course hes very careful. Sealed containers. When there are no students around of course.

That easy, eh?

Yeah. I mean, thats what it says in the book.

Interesting. An he dumps this stuff in the guys coffee, eh?

Right. He knows where the man eats lunch and just gets behind him and pours it in. Doesnt take much.

Does he get away with it? The guy dies I guess.

Oh yeah, the guy dies. No one knows what happened. He just gets sick and dies.

So, does this assassin screw up and go to the funeral or something and somebody spots him? Wait…he gets some on his hands and does himself in. Is that how it works out?

No. At least not yet. I mean, I havent finished it but so far the guy who does it is still alive. Still anonymous.

Well, so far so good, eh? How far into the book are you?

Oh…about half I guess.

So this guy still has plenty of time to screw up, eh? Usually some little thing he never noticed, you know how that goes. Success goes to his head and he becomes careless, or he gets involved with a woman. Always a major disaster in those situations. Especially the movies, boy those broads cause more trouble.

Well, so far theres no woman involved…in the book I mean.

So this guy that gets killed is a real prick, is that it?

Oh yeah, hurt a lot of people.

Hows he do that, a shylock or something?

Shylock?

You know, loan shark.

Oh, no. He worked for the VA. Made the lives of thousands of vets miserable, denying them their benefits, that sort of thing. Really horrible person. You really get to hate him.

Yeah, a lotta those bums need killing. Glad to hear somebodys writing a book about those bastards.

Me too. I/ll probably get to finish the book soon.

Let me know how it turns out—want another one?

Huh? Oh no. Thats plenty for me. I can actually feel it. Have to get home.

Right. Have a nice day.

You too.

Here we are, half a block and Im home. Bartenders hear all kinds of stories…Im sure. Never see him again. Even if suspicious. Flimsy story. Easy to check. No connection. Thats probably it. Nothing to do with a guilty conscience. Pressure. Feeling of accomplishment. Need to tell someone. Ego. Thats what it is. All ego. Bragging not confessing. Priests cant tell. Dont even know whos talking. Cant see. Could tell a priest and be safe. Insane. Cant trust them. Trust a politician for gods sake. Water. Oh, that tastes good. Dont think I was ever that dry. Dont feel like working. Still a little restless. Not like before though. Guess the walk took the edge off. Starting to feel a little weird…deflated I guess. Im okay. Dont know what to do now. Feel like something. Maybe a movie. No, that doesnt sound inviting. Nothing to think about. Or plan. Yeah, I guess thats it. Its sort of over. Dont feel like its over. Something unfinished…lacking. Really feel at loose ends. Oh god, cant even think of turning that on. Dont know what in the hell to do with myself. Okay, lets look at this. Couple of months my energy was focused on Barnard and now thats all over. But no closure. Yeah, that simple, no closure. Its over…hes over… The entire situation is history. There is nothing more to be done. Hes not around anymore. No need to ever think of him. He will not antagonize anyone anymore. Thats a good thing. Very good thing. A lot of vets are going to be happy when they find out. Would like to invite them all to dinner and tell them. See their faces. The huge smiles. Listen to the jokes. The cheers. All the Barnard stories…and then the son of a bitch did this…and that… Yeah…satisfaction. Thats missing. Need closure to have it. You work so hard to achieve something, then you succeed and its like theres no reason to live. As if they gave me a watch and retired me. People live and retire. My life is not without purpose now that this…this…situation is over. Thats insane. Remain anonymous. Funeral parlors filled with people. But who would notice? Lot of strangers. Family doesnt know co-workers. Keep head down. Talk to no one. Could wear a big mustache. And wig. Who would—thats nuts. Absolutely no connection. Wig and mustache. Madness. Too easy to check places that rent those things. Theatrical supplies. Its food poisoning. What could be more suspicious than buying a wig and mustache? Just go and look at the dearly departed. Dont sign the book. The book of the dead. Dead. Thats right. Barnard is dead! Hes not a dearly departed. He is not a deceased. No demise. He is not out to lunch. He is dead! Dead in the water. Very simple. Barnard is dead. No euphemism. Oh I am glad that youre dead you rascal you. Need to see him dead in his box. Oh poor Barnard, I knew him well Horatio. Yes, a light dinner and a visit to the motel of last resorts. Not a short term vacation. Death is so permanent. Dead. Its all over. Done with. Over and done with. Thats all there is there aint no more. Except for the dearly surviving. Its okay Crip, dont cry ol fella. My mother had four more children after me, Eenie, Meanie, Minie and Jack. Jack? What happened to Moe? She didnt want no Moe. Better keep Crip away from the cemetery. It will be fine. Nothing to worry about. Just go for a few minutes and leave. Can always eat later. Not hungry. Gut feels empty, but not hungry. Really not so bad. Feeling sluggish again. Ass dragging. Really at loose ends. Damn, this is ridiculous. Could always have a cup of coffee. Maybe stop off and get some ice cream. Something. Damn. Dont know what I want. Hell with it. Just go. Its not foolish. Arsonists always show up at their fires. Love them. I dont love Barnard and I am not an arsonist. Time to get going. Come on, lets go.

Beautiful night. Balmy breeze. Good night for a convertible. Open windows fine. Feels great. Hope theres no problem parking. Didnt think of that. May be a lot of people going there from work. We/ll see. Must be parking within walking distance. Thats possible. Might be like last child leaving home and the mother feels lost. Unfocused. Could very well be. Not that I feel so terrible. Just sort of adrift. Really had something to focus on…for months. Now only work. Antsy. Feel like flooring it and barreling through the night. Sense of speed with windows open. Noise. Feel the wind on my face. Better park here. Only half a block away, and who knows if theres anything closer. Well, here goes… Nice trees. That oak looks very old… Whoa, gut really bubbling. Like its trying to stop me. Maybe I am making a mistake. Who knows. Parking lots filled. Cant all be for him. Still plenty Im sure. Here goes… Jesus, it feels like a mortuary. BARNARD… Room C. This way… Like I thought, a lot of people. Just go in. Look solemn. Head bowed. Look no one in the eye. Dont have to mingle. Dont stay still too long. Someone will come over. No familiar faces. Or voices. Over the phone? Dont think so. Quiet anyway. Slowly toward the front. Not a bad casket. Shiny anyway. Stuffy in here. Its cool but I feel warm. Dont have to stay too long. Its okay. Feel alright. Not too bad actually. Quiet. No hysteria. No one there. Should go take a look. There he is. Dead. Give me a D E A D Dead! Its really him, Barnard. And hes no more. Deceased. Departed. Go to big Tipi in sky. Doesnt look too good. Knock, knock, any body home? Youre a real dead beat now Barnie. Guess I should move so someone else can look atim. Just one more minute.

He may wink at me. May all be a joke. He may suddenly jump up and start singing, 'Heaven, Im in heaven'... If youre in Heaven somethings wrong. Its all a cheat. The deck is marked, the game is crooked. Better move. People may be looking. Drift over there out of the way. Can still see him. Make sure he doesnt try to get away. You have to stay put Barnie, its not Halloween. There you are. You are really dead. Put them all together they spell DEAD, a word that means the world to me. Im not breathing but air keeps coming in...and going out. Should move soon. Someone wi—

Did you know Harry long?

Huh...(Harry? What????) Oh. (Harry) A few years. From the office.

Ive been his neighbor for 10 years. Fine man. Wonderful family man. Really a beautiful family. So tragic.

Yes. (hows ol Crip) Terrible. Im not sure I know exactly what happened. Ive been on vacation.

Oh, I see. Really tragic. So sudden. Came home from work, sick, a couple of days ago with food poisoning. And suddenly he was dead. So tragic.

You never know, do you?

No, you certainly do not. In the best of health one minute, and the next...

When its your time theres no avoiding it.

Never had a sick day in his life. Never missed a days work. Then out of nowhere his life is snuffed out.

Theres just no way of figuring these things.

So true—Oh excuse me, theres Maxwell. I need to speak to him. Pleasure.

Indeed.

Yes, indeedy deedy do. A modern day tragedy. The price we pay to maintain our civilization. The pace of life is much too fast. Food is grown fast, prepared fast, eaten fast, and periodically theres a bit of neglect in the mix and the first thing you know someone has food poisoning. Hear about that sort of thing all too often. Yes indeed. Something should really be done about it. Inspect those places more often, more thoroughly. God only knows how long they have dead meat hanging around. Gets into the grain of the wood, the sinks, floors, walls, pots, pans are covered with bacteria. Perfect environment for disease. I tell you it is criminal how these conditions are allowed to exist. I bet thousands die each year from these forms of contamination, but you dont hear about it. They keep it all hushed up. Thats the way big business is. All they care about is their bottom line. We are mere chattel to them, just consumers. But if they keep killing us off like this there wont be any consumers left. We should all write to our Congresspeople, letters to the editor, TV, radio, deluge them with letters, let them know we are aware of what is happening and we wont tolerate it any longer, we demand that steps be taken to ensure that we can stop in for a simple lunch and survive the food. Look at this man, cut down in the prime of life by someones negligence. Look at the survivors, the wife and children, and his dear dog, Crip, who even now has already gone days without food and will soon be as dearly departed as his master. This is not a game, yet you are taking a chance when you eat lunch. Perhaps we all need to go back to the old lunch pail and thermos. May not be chic, but it would be safer. It is absolutely—Ahh, that air feels good. There definitely was something dead about the air in there. No pun intended. Oppressive atmosphere. But he is dead. Gone the way of all flesh. Oh, I feel so much better now. It is not all a fantasy, it is as real as death can get. Hes dead. Maybe the next guy will be as rotten, but this one isnt going to screw anyone any more. God, I have such a powerful sense of accomplishment. Ive accomplished a lot as an engineer. Problems to solve. Staying focused. But this was so different. This was so much more real, so tangible. There was nothing theoretical about this. The problem was concrete as were the actions and the result. Engineering problems are interesting, fascinating, challenging, doing things that had never been done before. No small thing. No indeed. But this…this has been done so many times before it is beyond calculation. There was Adam and Eve, and there was Cain and Abel. Thats a long time ago and weve been doing it ever since. I have joined an ancient fraternity. I have killed a man. With my ingenuity, knowledge, courage, and my very own hands I have killed a man. I did not push a button, or spray impersonal bullets over an area, I, in fact, bit the bullet and addressed the problem head on and personally killed a man. I did not dispatch him, nor did I terminate him, eliminate him, I very simply killed him face to face. No euphemism, no second hand death. Just as I stand here and look myself in the eye in this mirror, I looked at him and did what was necessary to end his life. I killed the son of a bitch. Of course I did not look into his eyes as he was dying and tell him I was taking his life, but I dont have to get wrapped up in that, it is enough to know that he is dead and will not visit his evil upon anyone ever again. Never again! Hes still laying there in that box. He will never leave it. A true sense of permanency. Everyone goes home. No one checks up on him. He/ll be there in the morning looking as he did today. Guess they touch up his makeup. Could go back tomorrow and see. Might not be a good idea. Someone might realize I was there today. That one guy did talk to me. Forget it. All of it. Suddenly feel exhausted. Hungry. Make a sandwich or something.

And now he once again sleeps the sleep of the innocent. A gentle smile on his face and a body free of tension, twisting and turning. When he awakens it will be a new day. What it will bring is unknown to him at this moment. The day will bring with it exactly one day of living and he will do as he will with it. It is all up to him.

Ohhh, feel exhausted...doesnt seem very early...bright...slept all night...whats the time...lets see wow...slept almost nine hours, should be bouncing up and around...no sense...nine hours, shouldnt feel so sluggish...better get to the bathroom...eyes dont want to stay open...watch where Im peeing anyway...god, cant stop yawning...lights attacking my eyes...crazy, nuts, want to go back to bed. Should I? Got something? Pick up a bug? Just shower. Always works. Ohhh, all I do is yawn. What the hell. Cant drown in the shower. I hope. May yawn myself to death. Can die in the shower. Keep yawning and slip. Crack my head. Dumb way to die. Maybe some food and coffee will do it. Something has to. Cant make it like this…weak and hollow. Can hardly get my clothes on. Going to get lock jaw from yawning. Cant really be this tired. Not going back to bed. Dont care. Coffee will help. And food. Couldnt even make instant coffee, if I had any. Walk to the deli will help… Dont know. Just the thought is overwhelming. Well, not going to fix anything here. Obviously. Damn, eyes are tearing from yawning. Drive to the deli. Oh god, feel like a fool driving those couple of blocks. Obscene. Yeah, not going to get there any other way. Dont get there I dont eat. Need to eat. Can feel it. That may be all thats wrong. Sun spots or something. I dont know. Sometimes you wake up like this. Craving need for food. Feel so disconnected. Separated sort of. Felt so solid…so…whole last night. Dont get it. Ten hours ago I felt light…capable. The thought of moving is unbearable. Lifting a foot, moving a leg, then putting the foot down then going through the same things over and over my god its impossible. Cant do it. Feel like I weigh a ton. Too much weight to move. Have to drive. Maybe park around the corner. Driving will wake me up. Better. Damn, better stop yawning while driving. Could pile into someone and not even know it. Only two blocks. Thats where most accidents happen, they say. Couple blocks from home. Nobody will know I drove from home. Dont know where I live. Even so, I could be coming from somewhere else. Keep my eyes open. And alert. Just dont yawn. Stay al—terrific, just a few feet away. Ahh, made it.

Didnt yawn once. Lets hope its stopped. Dont want to yawn in the waitresses face. Thats ugly. Truly gauche. Oh god, out of nowhere. Guess I/ll just have to keep rubbing my eyes or nose or something. Keep my head down. Oh god, it wont stop. Its like being back in school. Everyone looking at you when you yawn and that damn Mizz Bubblehead or whatever her name was, 'If you tried sleeping at night maybe you would not be yawning in every ones face.' God, everyones face. Sat in the back of the room. Practically wrapped my arms around my head. What a bitch. Wonder why she hated me? Always singling me out for some damn thing. Nothing actually. Just liked to pick on me. Make me stand in front of the class. Recite something. She knew I hated to do that. She did it on purpose. Liked to see the pain in my eyes. Yeah. Thats why she made me stand next to her desk to recite. Everyone looking at me. Some of the guys, especially John and Wilson, would make faces and try to get me to laugh. Almost wet my pants once. Some friends. Did it every time. Couldnt seem to avoid looking at one of them. Different sides of the room. Could feel my face twisting in knots trying not to laugh and recite. Mizz Bubblehead looking at me, tapping her finger on the desk. Just staring. Could feel those eyes burning right through me. And the girls…oh god. Whispering behind their hands…giggling… and Sally Landry sitting in the front row, right in front of me, and she was getting boobs. All were really, but she had these…boobs… I could feel the sweat rolling down my back and sides and I had to recite or read some dumb poem for Bubblehead and I/d lose my place looking at

Sallys boobs and feeling weird all over oh god, why in the hell am I remembering this nonsense. Just nod my head, mumble, rub my eyes and nose, cover my face with my handkerchief, dont know whats happening, keep smiling, always smiling then they dont ask whats wrong, god thats annoying, if youre not smiling they want to know whats wrong, just keep smiling, but cant around Mizz Bubblehead, or while looking at Sally Landrys boobs. Especially Sallys boobs. Forgot all about my face then. Dont think I yawned while watching her walk across the room. Werent very big, but they were definitely boobs. Funny how these things change—krist, the handkerchief, shes looking right at me, lousy thing to do to someone while theyre eating, yawn, they look up from their food and see your wide, gaping mouth, your tongue and all that funny looking stuff under your tongue (at least its not like that black flappy stuff dogs have), your cavities, your fillings, all those funny little things hanging down in the back, oh god, thats beyond gauche, just cant do that to some one. Maybe I was on alert when I watched Sally, thats why I didnt yawn. Yeah, it is funny the changes, youre a little kid and other kids make fun of you by saying you go out with girls. Do not. Do so. Do not. Not. Not. Then in no time at all instead of being a sissy if youre seen talking to a girl, youre a sissy if you dont. Guess thats kind of how the world is, cant win. Maybe break even. Sallys boobs fascinated me. Wanted to just stare at them and see if I could see them growing. Dont think I made any connection with boobs and anything else. Just wanted to spend all my time staring at them.

Lets see if that food will work. Wake me up. Stop yawning. O krist, no good. Guess I/ll have to keep thinking of Sallys boobs on the way home so I wont yawn. Wonder what brought that up? When the hell was the last time I thought of Sally or her boobs? Not that they were really boobs yet. A year or so later they were. Dont seem to remember them particularly then. They all had them by then. No time for yawning in those days. Haha, we all became athletes, first base, second base. Closest I came to being a ball player. Took me long enough to learn to play that form of baseball. Cant say I was very proficient. Who knows how many were. We all lied to each other, or at least took liberties with the truth. Wonder if they wonder about all that? Well, home and no mishaps. Sallys boobs got me through breakfast. What now. God, this is dreadful. Unbearable inertia. Shouldnt have plopped on the couch. May never get up. If Sallys budding boobs helped maybe something more mature will help. Hell, who am I going to call? Dont even feel like picking up the phone. Make a date for tonight or the weekend and who knows how in the hell I/ll feel? Get stuck spending a night with someone youre bored with. Dont have to spend the night. But thats always expected. Even if they dont want to, or cant, they get upset if you dont want to. So you have to play the game and suppose its not a game, they just say, Lets go. Your place or mine? Terrific. What do I do, yawn in their face? Or ask them if they can shrink their boobs for a while? One way ticket to the asylum. Why bother, its all so pointless. You go to bed, make love for a few hours, get up in the morning and youre still faced with the first day of the rest of your life. What good is a diversion? Postponing the inevitable. Suppose I could work for a while. Why? Even if I could get up how in the hell do I walk all the way to my office, turn on the machine, review my work, see what has to be done, look—impossible. Got to breakfast. Thats it. Maybe for the week. Dont have to eat every day. The thought of eating is nauseating. Howd I get to breakfast? Oh god, my bodys feeling heavier and heavier. Dragging me down. Everything feels so black. What the hell is happening? Cant be happening again. Cant feel like that. I got past that. Life cant do that to me again. I wont let it. I wont tolerate it. Just put on the television. No need to get strangled by all this. Television. See what? A bunch a buildings get blown up. People blasted. Some asshole in uniform yelling, GO GO GO!!!! God, what drivel. Eliminate the violence, the special effect, the noise, and all you have are opening and closing credits. Yeah, sure. No thanks. Last thing I need is a fuzzy feelgood movie. If ol Shep got ripped apart and eaten by a mountain lion I/d feel good. No point in the boob tube. Ahhh, the way they toss them around its depressing. As if the boobs have a life of their own and some inane broads only reason for living is to shake them in your face. No wonder this country is going down the tubes. Average set is on 6 hours a day. Country of idiots. Its not a moral degeneration. A case of becoming amoral. Immorality is tangible. Its a definite mind set. It is a tangible perception of life and the actions needed to beat life at its own game. Immorality is not wishy washy. It is not fuzzy feelgoody.

Fundamentalists have a very definite agenda they pursue and it is tangible. Concrete. The boob tube softens the suckers up for them. They dont know it. They sit and get consumed by this mediocrity and swear to god theyre having fun ah, the hell with it. Its pointless. Yeah, sure, watch a Dodger game. Sit through hours of heart pounding excitement just to find out they lost, again. Now thats really an exercise in futility. Once every 5 minutes or so somebody throws a ball and someone else tries to hit it with a club. Oh how exciting. Now they both walk around in circles, bang their shoes, scratch their balls, adjust their hats, look around, shrug, shake, wiggle, then go through the entire scenario again…and again…and again…*ad infinitum, ad nauseum.* Well, at least they get to sit in the sun for hours, then spend a few more hours in traffic after the game is over. Whooppeee. A marble championship would be a lot more fun. Wonder if they still have them? Probably. Somewhere. Kids enjoy them. Maybe one of the last things they get to enjoy as kids. Not long before theyre thrown into the competition of the world. Dont just go to school and do your best. Must excel. Should excel at everything. But at least one thing anyway. They dont tell you what a horror story life is. How futile. Meaningless. Make money. God, nothings easier than making money. Then what? It crushes you. Life just gets heavier and heavier and envelopes you in its tentacles until it has squeezed all life from you but you dont die. You linger. Deeper and deeper into darkness. Grotesque delirium. Constant derision. Sunlight mocks you. Moonlight mocks you. Flowers, mockingbirds, trees, shadows mock you. Street lights are on. To guide or mock? They push back the darkness, yet it is always there waiting to crush you. The sun shatters the darkness but the sun gives up in despair. The darkness always rebounds and returns to block out the light of the sun, to send it down, down, out of sight, whimpering before the black night. The darkness always follows, falls, descends. Always. We get our moment in the sun. But only a moment. Feeling energized by it, ignited, illumined, radiant, lighted, see our path so clearly, no questions, no doubts, so clearly and so definitively marked it is almost unnecessary to watch where you place each foot, they simply go where they need to go, moving you forward deeper into the light, the single purpose of the light, light the bringer of life and then you know… Yes! You know. This is *the* life you were created for. This is the reason you bother to breathe in and out. It all makes sense. No, the mysteries of life are not solved. They are unimportant. Merely toys to be played with, then cast away or passed on as is done with childrens toys. Yet we know the children are playing with toys. We believe we are concerning ourselves with the most important questions life presents. Ahhh, the mysteries. You can study the mysteries, discuss them, analyze them, debate them, belittle them, canonize them, or…or you can live life. Ahh, why bother even thinking about it? You have your moment of sublime purpose, appointment. Receive the blessing of Sanction and experience your entire being being bathed in light. The supreme and exquisite joy of not having to drag the body around, of moving it from here to there. Rather, it seeming to simply move itself where it needs to go, where it can best serve the needs of life. Yet life eventually casts you aside as if it were a corporation. Go. Leave. Never darken this door again. You are no longer needed or wanted. How does this happen? Why does this happen? Its as if I didnt have that time in the light. The heavy, impenetrable darkness starting to crush me again in the wink of an eye. Oh god, feels like my shoulders are wrapped around my hips. Feel so twisted and curled. How did I end up back here? At least I do have the gun now. I do have the ability to break this chain. There is that. I do not have to be a victim. I do not have to be abused by life. I can take that one assertive step that we all have a right to take. What they say is immaterial. I can certainly do it if I so choose. It is my life. Not theirs. What do I care about their stupid laws? They can control my life, but not my death. That is my choice. Yes, so true, knowing I have that choice, and *right*, and, of course, the means whenever I choose, takes away that sense of urgency. There is no enforced waiting period. Everything is in my hands. To be or not to be. It is a question I can answer whenever I choose. It is all up to me. Perhaps I can sleep. I think so. Feel weary. And so, so tired. Worn out. I could just stretch my legs out and sleep here. No. Wouldnt work. Wake up in the middle of the night, unable to go back to sleep. Thats unbearable. Have to cut a hole in the darkness to breathe. I can force myself up now, now that I know I can do whatever I choose, when I choose. It is all up to me. Well, we/ll see what the morrow brings.

Argh…damn sunlight. Feels like someone is pressing on my eyeballs…their thumbs. Hot. Must be late. Could never get back to sleep. Cant open my eyes. The sunlight. Why should I open my eyes? Same old shit. The window, the blinds, the curtains, the sunlight, the wall, the goddamn birds, another hopeless day oh god. Yeah, have to get up sooner or later. Piss in the bed. What the hell. Better than getting up. That starts the day. Stay in bed. No day. No nothing. Stay in bed eventually go back to sleep. Cant stay in bed. Cursed to get up. Cant piss in bed. Ah hell, maybe I will be able to go back to bed… No good. Screw a shower. Maybe it will do something. I dont know. Just the thought is so tiring…take off the pajamas, open the shower door, turn on the water, adjust the temperature…oh god, on and on and on, endless…then soap up…pick up the soap, over your entire body, lift your goddamn legs, each and every little thing impossible, cant even think of it, do it all over then dry your whole goddamn body, oh god…cant lean against this door forever. In or out. Just stand under the water. My legs want to fold. Easy, just hold on. Water does feel good. Whats the point? Still have the whole day to get through…yeah, then another and another and another and on and on…how many days can you take like this? Why bother with this whole mess? Dont even feel like going to Barnards funeral. Not allowed to enjoy yourself. Dont let life see youre happy. Slam dunk! Whammo. This is the Pit and the Pendulum. Its wet, if nothing else. Can

I dissolve? Just go down the drain with the water? How long can you just stand here? Its own lethargy. Hypnotic. Am I slowly sliding? Turn around? How? Inch my hands along the sides and hope I dont slip? Little bit at a time? Little more…more…damn, its pounding in my ear…little more…little more…ohhh, that feels good…let it pound my back…how long can I lean against the back like this? I/ll end up sliding down and whacking my head. Stupid way to die. But I would be dead! Wouldnt even know it. Just clunk my head on the wall. Maybe bleed. Could even drown. Fat chance. Be unconscious for a while, water wake me up. Head hurt. Huge lump. Sick. I fell in the shower doctor. Sure, need that kind of humiliation on top of everything. Am I sliding? Water seems to be numbing me. Guess it did feel good…for a while. Gets boring. Water logged. Knew it was stupid. Now I have to turn around again. Not all the way. Reach around and turn off the water.Yeah…that makes it easier. Just breathe for a minute… In… Out… Guess I am awake. Oh well, no chance of sleeping anyway. Ohhh… Slide the damn door open. Jesus, Im so weak. Too much water…dissolved my energy. Comeon, open you…get my hand in here…shove…my god, I can hardly move it…oh no, cant. Too big, too heavy. Air dry. Sure is hot enough. Maybe I can get into the robe…ah no, the hell with it. Big deal, drip on the rug. Wow, really weak. Better sit. Yeah, the whole days ahead. Then another night. Might not sleep tonight. Watch TV? Might put me to sleep? Read a book. Something. Cant get dressed how am I going to get through the day…every endless minute. God, so bright need sunglasses in the house and I feel so black. How can this be? Survived this once. What happened? Howd I get back here? Isnt once enough? It was bad enough then. This is so much darker. To go back into the darkness after being in the light is beyond torture. Must be a god, man isnt capable of such a plan. Too much to control. Too many circumstances. Man cant bring about such inner peace. No. God surely is. Why? Why does this happen? Ahhh, whats the use. Least dont have to wait. Have to get dressed first. Cant shoot yourself naked. How the hell am I going to get dressed? Get the gun? Cant think of moving. Got in the shower, can get the gun. This is ridiculous. Going to sit here naked all day? The rest of your life? At least have some dignity. Heads going to be blown off, least the rest can be presentable. Yeah. Live fast and all that. How do you make a good looking corpse with the top of your head blown off? Its all so stupid. Living, dying. All stupid. So purposeless. Why suffer? Get it over with. Want to sit here, like this, day after day? Maybe for years? What the hells so difficult about putting on some clothes? Done it all your life. Yeah, all my life. Jesus, Im depressed not paralyzed. How stupid can you be? Sitting around naked isnt going to change anything. Yeah… Yeah. Shit! What does it take, 2 minutes? Grab some old khakis… So wacky. A shirt over my head, slide my feet into some shoes. Thats it. Now the gun. Feels good. Looks good. Clean. Sit here for a minute. Why did I wait so long? Feel better already. Know Im not trapped. I have my way out. Can use it anytime I want. Just stick it in my mouth...argh, does taste nasty. Well, not too bad actually. Just a little oily...metallic. Pull the trigger and the taste is gone. Push it actually. Must be something I want to do first. Must have a last request. Yeah...I want to die. I have to die. This will never change. Always feel like this. Cant work. Just sit here and wait to put the barrel in my mouth and pull the trigger. Its all I have to look forward to. My only purpose left. To leave the top of my head on the ceiling. Theres no alternative. Just a matter of time. Inevitable. Cant stand the crushing burden. Of living. Its not living. Living is fine. This darkness of being alive without being able to live is inhuman. I couldnt even wish it on Barnard. Every lousy breaths an eternity. Sit for hours and its only minutes. Struggle to breathe...for what? To struggle. Pointless. Dont know how air gets in. Cant breathe. Wonder how many people will die in this heatwave? Lucky. Theyre free. Dont have to force their way through this madness. Why cant I pull the trigger for gods sake? Oh shit. Cant keep sucking on this thing. Mouth tastes like shit. Just my luck I/ll break my teeth on it. Have to keep trying. One of these times I/ll just pull it and it will be over. I hope. It better be. No, of course not. None of that church stuff. But dont know. Cant be. Cant take your pain with you. That degree of cruelty is beyond imagination. No one...nothing could be so...so... Not even a Barnard. What is he doing now? Is he just dead, or paying for his sins? Dead is dead. At least I know what Im doing. Yeah. I have a purpose. To die. Maybe thats the only purpose. Who knows. Its the purpose of my life...now, today. To die. Something to live for. Yeah, that is weird. Funny. But true. Help get thru the day. Dont feel so hopeless…or helpless. Thank god I got this gun. Im not at the mercy of some evil demon. I can end it. When I choose. Thats enough. To live for. Up to me. No one else. I am in control of my life. Almost feel like working. Maybe later. Might eat. Something in the freezer. Think legs feel lighter. Guess been sitting here all day. Be night soon. Slept last night. Can probably turn on the TV. Later. Make me tired. Might be something decent on. Movie. Oldie. THE KILLING. Ohhh, DRACULA. Lugosi. No chance. Possible. Festival or something. No, not now. Halloween. Probably LASSIE, or OLD YELLER. Eechh, drivel. At least not ITS A WONDERFUL LIFE. Spared that. Kill the TV. Just before I kill myself. Maybe it will burn in hell. Cant look through the TV Guide. Jesus. Insane. Find it. Pick it up. Read it. Actually go through the pages. Just run through the channels. Take time to suck on the barrel of this thing. Trigger just a few inches away. Fascinating. Snake and bird. Cant see it. Only my thumb. How long can I stare? Starting to blur. Burn. Couple of them. Keep staring…many guns…only guns. Only feel one mouth. Would only feel one bullet. Will I feel it? How long? Maybe nothing. Dead before pain registers. Could be. Dont taste it any more. Not really. Like a smell. Soon you dont notice. Its a taste. Nothing. Just a taste. Not good, not bad. Can ignore it. Gets absorbed. Everything fades eventually. Peanuts. Asparagus. Dont keep eating. Stop for a second at least. Put more in mouth. Get tired of chewing eventually. Jaws. Teeth. Stomach fills. Always have to stop. Eventually. Just suck the barrel. Just in the mouth. No effort. Yeah…I guess. Baby and pacifier. Fall asleep with it in mouth. Will I fall asleep with this in my mouth? Weird. If I twitch. Slight spasm. Boom. Fall asleep sitting up always jerk up. Could pull the trigger. If I sit here like this, long enough, it just might happen. Just like that. Over. Jaws getting tired. Almost as bad as the dentist. Cant sit like this for ever. Know that. Can try. See if trigger gets pulled. Yeah, too heavy. Probably just drop it. God, goes off and shoots me in the leg. Howd I explain that? This wont work anyway. Just get used to having it in my mouth. Damn, now I can taste it. My jaw is creaking. Oh well, just put it on the couch. Arm tired. Am hungry. Almost dark. Late. Yeah, short distance to kitchen. Just check out the freezer. Stick something in the microwave. Grab anything. Pot luck. Later. No TV now. Get this thing cooking. If I can read the directions. Funny, just pushing the buttons Im getting really hungry. True, long time. Still, twice as hungry as was before pushing the buttons. Could put it on a plate and pretend its a real meal. Why bother? Will have to wash the plate. Sooner or later. This is fine. Oh well, its food. Kill the hunger. They always this salty? Maybe that gun oil makes it seem saltier. Oh well… Feels good to move my jaws. Need the exercise. Get muscles in my right hand and jaws. Feels weird…light and achy. Have to keep my arm from flying off into space. Get the circulation back. Been sitting there for hours. No wonder my arm feels so weird. Exercise of eating will help. Yeah, eating keeps you alive. Need to stay alive to kill myself. Like that convict in Sing Sing. Osning on the

Hudson…Riverview Estates. When? Maybe the thirties. Tried to kill himself a few hours before supposed to be electrocuted. Rushed him to the hospital in town, called in specialists, saved his life, then rushed him back to Sing Sing in time to be killed. Makes a lot of sense. Like everything else in this world. Wonder if they indicted him for attempted suicide before they killed him? Cant remember where I read that. Some detective magazine I guess. Couldnt just let the poor son of a bitch die. No. *They* had to kill him or it wouldnt be fair…or some crazy thing. Justice. Thats what they yell about, justice. Hypocritical slimes. They just enjoy killing. They know it doesnt do any good, doesnt stop people from killing. They just enjoy it. Got to find someone to punish or life isnt worth living. Krist, the persons in jail, they cant hurt anyone. On the outside anyway. Just leave them there. If they left him alone he would have died anyway. Yeah, maybe on time…at the stroke of 12 midnight. Ahh, forget it. No point in going crazy. Dyings one thing, going crazys another. May not have to worry about pulling the trigger. TV dinners may kill me. No wonder Americans are so unhealthy, living on this garbage. Yeah…and McDonalds. Jesus, what kind of tastebuds do they have? Do they have any? Raised on potato chips and soda I guess you dont have any tastebuds by the time youre old enough to cross the street by yourself. Give them a tasty, healthy meal and they get sick. Need polluted garbage. Like fresh air…itll killem. Now theres a great idea. New form of warfare. Kill the population with fresh air and good food. It would work. What would happen to the mafia if they couldnt endlessly smoke those cigarettes and guinea ropes and drink espresso? They would fall like leaves in autumn. Gagging, strangling, gasping. Why didnt the FBI think of that? The OCD. New anti-crime weapon. To torture them make them drink American coffee and smoke ultra-lights, double filtered, imitation cigarettes. Theyd all confess to anything, even the Kennedy assassination. One way to get rid of the conspiracy theories. Even the Inquisition didnt think of that. Forgive me father for I have sinned. I have had impure thoughts.

Youre damn right you did. Who doya think you are, eh, talking likea that?

Mea culpa father.

You betcha ya sweet ass.

Mea fucking culpa.

Thaza right. Go say somea Hail Marys an Lordsa Prayer. An put a bundle inna the poor box—hey, neva mine, justa give it to me, somea bodys always a rippin off the poor box.

Thank you father. Yes father.

Oh yeah, remember, no beatin off.

Gotya padre.

Yeah, sure, I gotya. There really isnt anything to believe in. Not out there. Governments? At best theyre despicable. Yeah, deshpicable. At their very best, the ultimate good, theyre hypocritical. Constantly killing and pillaging because its good business, its good for the *Bottom Line*, the holy grail of capitalism. Never allow anything like the welfare of people to stand in the way of

Corporate profits. Comeon, be real, what do the lives of a few million people mean if they get in the way of our…bow your heads children…Bottom Line. And the church. The church! The goddamn church, THOSE RAT BASTARDS!!!! The only thing theyre good for is buggering (what a great word) young boys. I guess they save the little girls for the nuns. Why in the hell do I think of these things? I cant stand living in the rotten world. Why torture myself? Why do I keep looking around at the world and seeing it for what it truly is? The pain of living is unbearable under any circumstances, why do I aggravate myself like this? Jesus, Jesus, Jesus. Help me. Please, help me. If you really exist, you skinny jew bastard, help me kill myself. I know you didnt have the balls to do yourself in, you forced others to do it and their blood is on your hands. Pilate wanted you to just take a walk, but you refused, you forced him to turn you over to the mob and now they have to share the guilt of your death. Thats why you came back so soon, to atone for your sins…yeah, and you got a long time to do that. You not only forced all those people to become murderers, but you are responsible for Christianity, and the hundreds of millions upon millions of lives that have been destroyed. Still being destroyed. Every day. Every day! You have any idea what thats like? Do you? Do you even give a rats ass? You cant. Well, I hope you really are the big kahuna you claim to be. Yeah. Then you can feel the pain of all those hundreds of millions of souls you helped bring to the depths of despair and anguish. I dont know why I even talk to you. You are beyond loathsome. But Im still going to offer you the chance to atone, to do something for someone once in your life. Help me pull this trigger. Help me end my pain and suffering. Help me to get free of this life. This impossible life of anguish and misery. Do that for me and I will forgive you. I will give you absolution and you can get your skinny ass out of here. Youve got 24 hours jc. Thats it. 24 hours. And its your last chance for atonement. Grab it while you can. That big weasel in the sky must be pissed off at you and is probably getting ready to zap your ass. Which is fine with me, but that may be a long time in coming and I want to get out of this shit now…right now! I dont see why you should be allowed to continue to inflict pain and misery on the world. Seems to me its an offer you cant refuse. Youd better go for it jewboy, this special offer can not be repeated. Its a one time, one day offer. Now please, get outta here. I wouldnt want my friends to see me talking to you. Allowing street people in the house is one thing, but you… Ahhh, ate the whole tv dinner and Im still alive. Well, it took Barnard a while to die. Food poisoning doesnt happen instantly. Maybe tv dinners are part of the communist conspiracy. Hang the capitalists on their own petard. O krist, damn near midnight. Im still here. Shit! Well, no need to get depressed. May be able to kill myself tomorrow. Maybe I/ll die tomorrow. If I do, will it make me a plagiarist? O krist, around and around. All I do is sink deeper and deeper into the morass of misery. Cant live and cant die. The eternal and perpetual torture. That is always the essence and thrust of torture…the threat of death yet never bringing it about. Only pain… Only pain. In time its the promise of death that tortures. How did life get to be like this? Was it created this way? Seems that way. If you believe the bible. From the very beginning they were killing each other. Thousands and thousands of years before the jew boy. Christians are Johnnys come lately when it comes to murder, mayhem, raping and pillaging. They learned fast though. Givem credit. No worse than anybody else though. Ohh, so what? Whats the big deal? People always find a way to justify killing each other. Thats part of the foundation of all these religions, justification. Having your friend killed so you can grab his wife can be justified when you believe its in the name of god...or the devil made me do it. Either way. Create a belief system to justify the satisfying of your lust. Scared of homosexuals and women??? become a christian fundamentalist and believe god told you how evil they are so its just fine to kill them. Just dont get caught in a motel room with one...with your pants down. Naughty, naughty. O krist, guess I have to go to bed. Weary of all this. Weary. Thank god I didnt dirty a dish. Dont want dirty dishes around when they find me. Cant lift the damn gun. Wont shoot. Cant will it to...or my finger to pull. Better leave it here. Too exhausted. No accidental shots. When it goes off the barrels going to be in my mouth. Oh god...I/ll wake up. I know it. I/ll wake up. The demonsll be waiting. Like vultures. Drooling. Waiting. Silent. Ugly...beyond ugly...beyond grotesque. Beyond...beyond what? Cant take any more. Cant stand. Bodys warped. So weak. Couldnt lift it with two hands. Have to sleep. Cant stay awake. I/ll go mad. Devoured by demons. Gnawing through my skull. Sucking the fluid from my spine…the marrow from my bones. Dripping acid into my brain. The cries of tortured children in my ears. The ravages of cancer, the screams of the bloated bodies on the battle fields…every cry for help, every plea for mercy mauling my mind and clawing my heart oh god, is there no end to any of this? no beginning to erase? no light anywhere??? no glimmer for the dark recesses of my mind???? All under a bushel. Hidden away. Saved for another day. For yet another day…and another and another… Please…something, something…anything, somewhere. Mercy. I ask only to die. Is that so much? too much? Can such a request possibly be beyond reason? To just die. Thats all. Not wealth…or fame or power or…or adulation. Death. That is all. Death. Totally. Completely. Irrevocably. A simple request from a tortured soul. Repent jesus. Atone for your sins. How simple a request. No moving of mountains hence. No water to wine…fishes and loaves…no Lazarus coming forth. You brought your friend back. How selfish. Theres a body missing. In this huge vast scheme of madness theres a vacancy, a missing body. Dont you see what youve done? The universe is out of balance because of your selfishness. You wanted to keep your friend around, thats all you cared about. Yourself. Always you. You are all that matters. Look at the madness in the world, a world trying to fill that vacancy. How many more lives must needlessly be destroyed? I will fill that vacancy. I offer to bring balance back to this universe. I make no sacrifice. I do not claim martyrdom, as you did. I admit and accept my selfishness. Yet the need is there and I can fulfill it. Atone you hypocrite. Give up your self-centered self-aggrandizement. We can both be free. Allow me to die and be absolved of your sins. I ask…pray, that I will close my eyes and be cushioned tenderly by the darkness, and that the darkness will be eternal. Oh, its certainly a consummation devoutly to be wished. That is all I ask. No salvation. No eternal life. Just eternal darkness. Sweet, beloved darkness. Please…please, come to me…soothe me…enlighten me with the impenetrable blackness…blackness for this night and all eternity… Ahhh sweet black blessing… my heart beseeches…my arms await to embrace you, my mind hungers for your kiss. Kiss away my tears…soothe my tortured heart with your darkness.

And thus a sacred plea from the man as he experiences the anguish of the human condition. Have you not seen it everywhere, most especially within yourself? It is simply part of the dilemma…contradictions, vacillation, confusion, self-deception, he is but a man. Does it not move your heart to see how he struggles to stay in the darkness, doing all he can, yet again, to avoid acknowledging that another day is upon him, another day of consciousness, of being aware of the pain in every cell and fiber of his being? What excruciating pain emanates from his body as he tosses about, seeking that magic position that will allow him to go back into sleep, the merciful darkness he so treasures. A black sleepshade, ear plugs, hugging the pillow, any and every device that has ever worked at any time in his life. All for a few minutes more of sleep, yet in sleep a few minutes can be as hours, the only important thing being that you not awaken to the point of needing to get up, of having to once again face the day. He knows, as everyone does, that that moment will come, as always, yet what a treasure to postpone it as long as possible. Once up the inevitable follows. No flinging of sleepshade against the wall, no screaming at the light coming through the blinds, no shaking of fist at the world, just the simple recognition that another day has started, a day that may possibly bring to an end all his days. Yet I still think not. I have yet to see fault within the man. I say this even as he once again puts the barrel of the gun in his mouth, closes his eyes and tries to force his finger to pull the trigger. Another painful, boring day, pitiful and arduous. A day almost indistinguishable from the previous one, different only as each day is always new, the pain new yet old and endless.

Must look like a question mark. Head wont raise. Hanging like a melon. Krist, what the hell must I look like bent in half with a gun barrel in my mouth? Animals dont sit around with a gun barrel in their mouths. They live as long as they can. Follow their instincts and their instincts tell them to live. They dont think. Dont ponder or contemplate. They dont think and just live. I think therefore I die. But Im not dead. Im sitting here with a gun barrel in my mouth…not an oboe, not a recorder, nor a clarinet or even a penny whistle. I have been sitting here so long with this in my mouth its an extension of my tongue. I have been sitting here with this in my mouth so long it has effected a genetic change. What might take endless generations and centuries has been accomplished in the wink of an eye. If I were to sire a child at this very moment its natural tongue would segue into hollow tubing of gun metal. No way of knowing how long it would be. Inches…feet…who knows? All of it might not fit into the mouth. It might hang pendulously, clanging, perhaps, against the childs chest. What if I stay like this indefinitely, would the metallic extension of the tongue be attached to a hand? Would it look as if the hand were reaching into the mouth or reaching from the mouth? What sort of hideous monstrosity would be created? How would it eat? How is it possible to chew with your tongue hanging from your mouth or a gun barrel inserted into your mouth? Could it speak? Can I speak now? I cant understand what Im saying. I know what I want to say, but am I actually saying it? So it can be understood? If no one hears me am I speaking? Is my head hanging lower? Who can answer this for me? Who am I asking? I talk and talk and talk but say nothing. My head rumbles with words yet I am silent. I am tortured and agonized by words yet I remain mute. If the words were coming from outside I could parry them as with a foil and laugh and thrust, but I am immobilized by the words resounding and reverberating and slashing and stabbing in my head. Is it really the words that weigh me down so that my hand hangs ever further down my chest, the barrel going deeper—no, the barrel can not go deeper as the hand too goes lower, as it must. How deep can the barrel go before it is thrown out by retching? That can not be allowed. The barrel must always be strategically fixed in the mouth so even an accidental triggering will leave the back of my head imbedded in the wall. Sounds strange. But not gruesome. It will be for the onlooker. But I wont be seeing. I will simply be a wallflower. So, nothing changes. Even as death approaches and time runs out…nothing changes. Only appearances. Thank god I cant see me. Would I cry to see such a sad scene, a man trying so desperately to die he ends up looking like…like…like this, body bent, twisted, a gun barrel apparently a permanent part of his anatomy? Would I care and ask if I could help? Suppose I…the me sitting on the couch, said yes, please push my finger against the trigger. What would I do? Would I feel such profound compassion and empathy I would do as I request; or would I decline for fear of being a murderer? Dont know. Is that why I am unable to pull the trigger, I think I/ll be a murderer? No. A persons life is their own, their own to end if they want to. Period. Screw the church. And their purgatories and hells. The only reason I would want to avoid hell, if it exists, is that it is filled with them. Hell must be populated with the devout, the fundamentalist, the Barnards. I suspect when you die you die. When do I die? When do I die??? everyday, all day, yet death continually evades me. Pull damned finger. I dont think I can even pull this thing out. I have to pull the trigger or spend the rest of my life like this. I am spending the rest of my life like this. All I have to do is squeeze the trigger gently, just soft, easy squeeze. Ive done it on the range. Aimed and squeezed the trigger slowly. Had no trouble. All that practice to no avail. What the hell good is it to know what to do if you cant do it when needed? Its insane. I can take it apart and put it back together with my eyes closed. Cant pull the trigger. Finger just wont squeeze it. No strain. No pain. Just a squeeze. Im going to fall off this couch. Maybe then it will squeeze. My stomach is screaming for food. It needs more than the taste of gun metal. It needs more than thinking. More than air. It wants food. Fine. How do I fix something to eat with only one hand? Even tv dinner? Maybe I can pull it out with my other hand? Worse than yesterday. Muscles, joints locked. Late. Faint glow in sky, but not for long. Wish I wanted to eat. How can I be so hungry and not want to eat? Strange. No. Want to eat. Dont want to fix it. Put it in front of me. Not now. Maybe later. Why eat if Im going to die? All that trouble. Suppose I do get this out of my mouth and nuke a tv dinner, then half an hour later, or whenever, Im dead. All that work for nothing. Im crumbling. Arm and hand numb again. Didnt realize it. Maybe for hours. No wonder it couldnt squeeze. Do have to pull it out. My jaw seems locked. Teeth clamping down on it. Didnt know. For hours and didnt know. Have to grab my wrist with my other hand and—no. Break my teeth. Dont need that now. Feel bad enough. Lets see, what in the hell do…start with jaw. Yeah th—no, wait. Krist, cant think straight. How long have I been sitting here like this? Was still morning when I got up. Dark now. Must be after nine. Im frozen in this position. Like an old Indian curled over a campfire. First…first…what the hell is first? oh yeah, of course. Got to hang over couch. Make sure. Gun falls on couch. My god, everythings stiff. Okay, slow, easy does it, got to move slowly. Alright, thats it, lean against the back…now, massage jaws, got to massage slowly and keep trying to open mouth...yeah...oh yeah, its working, I can feel it o krist, I hope it doesnt crack. I hate it when it cracks. Feels like the end of the world. Just keep massaging slowly, move slowly, dont crack, please dont crack, just keep trying to open up, easy, easy, tiny little bit, just go slowly, its working...yeah, its moving, its actually moving, I can feel it, my jaw is moving, its opening my mouth, oh god, dont crack...nice and slow...yeah...its opening...dont think teeth are touching barrel...think...easy...easy...yeah, yeah...it is opening...okay, now...nice and easy...thats it, just hold the hand gently...firmly... Easy...easy...yeah...pull it out...little more...thats it...little more...pull your head away...good...good...its working...its working...almost out...good...oh, I think the teeth are free...no spasms in jaw...thank god...it hasnt cracked...hate that blinding pain...can feel the tip with my tongue...aaaaahhhhhhhhhh...just leave it on the couch...still cant move my jaw...okay...mouth will close in a minute...ooohhhhhhhhhhhh god, my arm is throbbing, jesus it hurts, blood must be pounding, oh jesus, o krist, rub it rub it inside the elbow...

well, it got me on my feet, but Im wobbly...jesus, I cant walk... I/ll be damned, sat there so long I cant walk....Well, just have to inch along one little step at a time...well...its working... damn...how the hell did I sit here so long I ended up like this...again? Its okay, its okay. Just dont give up. Might need the irony. Eat a hearty and nourishing tv dinner then kill myself. Didnt work yesterday. Okay. Edison never gave up. The Wright Brothers didnt give up. Just keep trying. Okay, the circulations back. Legs and arms move. Maybe some noise. Might help. Turn the TV on. Seems fair. Eating a tv dinner. They deserve each other. Both so aggravating I/ll forget how I feel. Yeah, do feel like a failure. Been sitting here for years trying to end the misery, to kill the pain, and keep failing. Cant give up. Yet Im getting so depressed I cant try. How did this happen? How did I get here…like this…feeling so bad I cant even kill myself? I dont feel good enough to kill myself. I am chewing. I can hear my jaw creaking. Moves so slow. Hard time lifting food to my mouth. Arm still feels like its detached. Not important. Keep chewing. Wake up the body. Chew…slowly…carefully…chew…chew. Cant even say its no good. Not important. Dont care. Whats the difference. Nothings important. Oh god, not again. How long? How long can it go on???? For ever. And ever. Im doomed to spend all my days sitting as I did today. Nights feeling as I do now. Blackness would be lighter than this. So far beyond hopeless. Oh god, I just cant take it…yet I know I will…will keep awakening to a new day…another day like all the others…beyond bleak…beyond black…beyond hope for change or relief. That is my destiny…my life…to keep living this day… I cant even try to fool myself that maybe tomorrow I will squeeze the trigger. I never will. Theres no point in trying. No point in sitting with it in my mouth hoping, praying I/ll be able to end all this and find some peace. It is all an illusion. A painful hoax. There is no hope for death. It isnt coming. Only endless dying. I can see that now. Oh so clearly. The hope I would eventually squeeze the trigger was just more deception. Oh god, what an indescribable bareness I feel. No words. They dont exist. Not for this. I just have to give myself up to the futility and bleak, crushing nothingness of my life…vacant of all meaning…oh god…how agonizingly despairing the simple truth…empty of purpose…yes…yes, so true, vacant of substance…nothing to resist…nothing to strive for…to wish for…to hope for…not even anything to defy…no battle of light and darkness, good and evil…no struggle for honor…most wretched of all, not even a fight against nothingness, no struggle for fulfillment…simply an absence of all sensibilities…only nothing…nothing…no fall from valor…no integrity to be reclaimed or perversion to be renounced…no…not even nothingness, but something so hideously beyond its almost ineffable…the total absence of everything, even nothingness… I—what??? what the hell they talking about? Thats a long time ago…

'…and it is estimated that at least 200 adults and more than 50 children attended the barbecue celebrating the event that occurred 30 years ago today and—'

I remember that. On the news for days.

'…as you can see there are tubs filled with ice and watermelons, and others with soda and beer—'

Wonder where the bourbon is? Off camera probably, oh god, theres a fiddler too.

'…and this has been an annual event since the verdict was returned 30 years ago, but today—'

Yeah, a day to remember…an extraordinary day. Another day of infamy.

'…so it is plain to see that no one is anxious or willing to speak with us, except for some of the young children who are just having fun at the barbecue and have no idea what is being celebrated—Oh here comes the man who—'

Jesus, look at him…at them. Theyre cheering and jumping up and down—

'…fathers are carrying children on their shoulders so they can get a better look at Big Jim Kinsey, who is walking around and shaking hands and slapping shoulders—Oh, some people are blocking the camera, Please, let us through, this is network news and—'

It really is Kinsey. Must have put on 50 pounds in the last 30 years, but its him. No doubt. Grinning from ear to ear. Those people idolize him…worship him. A real folk hero…

'Please… Please, let us through…let—Mr Kinsey would you say—please, let us—'

'Now, now, no need to be gettin itchy britches with these here TV folk, yuall just letem on through, we have to be hospitable so mind your manners—'

My god, they adore the man. They look like they want to kill those TV people…well, might not be such a bad idea. They are obnoxious. As a professional group, they certainly are lacking in basic human decency. Not as bad as lawyers and politicians, but they are not too far behind. Dangerous too when—

'Mr Kinsey, would you say a few words to our audience, sir?'

'Well now thats right neighborly of you—Now, now, Clyde, dont chuall go puttin that big ol han of yurs in front of the mans camera—Yuall have to be excusin ol

Clyde here, hes been my closest fren for fifty year...more, aint that right, Clyde? Hes a good ol boy, jus thinks I need protectin.'

'Damn right, you never know what these here—'

'No, no, Clyde, no need to be gettin all riled up.'

'Mr Kinsey, would you like to tell our audience the occasion for this barbecue and celebration every year for 30 years now?'

'I/ll tel—'

'Now. Clyde, just simmer on down. Ol Clyde here dont take kindly to people interfering in our business. You see, we/re just plain country folk...as you can see this is a small town but we are a proud people.'

My god, listen to them cheer. They look like Snopes family rejects and they act like the salt of the earth.

'...so we/re celebrating the victory of David over Goliath in—'

'David over Goliath?'

'Thats right, sonny. The David of small town America over the Goliath of a government that wants to tell us how to live and invade our homes and we said plain and simple, No sir Mr Federal Government, youre not telling us what to do. We been born free an by god we will die free!'

This is incredible. Never seen anything like this. They—

'Back to you.'

'Thanks, Steve. That was Steve Wilson at the 30th annual barbecue and picnic celebrating the acquittal of Big Jim Kinsey in the deaths of two black doctors who were part of the Medicare taskforce to desegregate hospitals. Their mutilated bodies were found just outside of town, in a ditch, and though there was ample evidence connecting Jim Kinsey to the crime, a jury took just a little more than an hour to acquit him. As you have just seen and—'

My god...a barbecue and picnic. Annual celebration. For thirty years. Everyone knows what happened. Everyone. They dont care—no, no, thats just it, they do care. Thats why theyre celebrating. They take pride in his actions... yeah, and hide behind it...them. All he did was what they wanted to do. Hes a hero. They couldnt do it, but he did do it. He was happy. Beaming. No remorse. No guilt. Beaming...and free. Those two dead men dont matter...they dont even exist. Innocent people trying to help other people. Wiped out...like...like chalk on a board...like a mistake...just wiped out. Erased. They eat barbecue, drink cold beer, sip whisky from a jug, laugh and hoot, slap their knees, each others shoulders, fiddlers scratch and whine and every body has a good ol time. Protecting their heritage. States rights. Listen to the evidence then adjourn to a room and talk about the weather, the crops, the fishing in the deep pool at Hastings Bend. Check their watches. From time to time. We are deliberating. Law and order. Fair and square. Overhaul Larrys tractor. Deweys pickup. Never seen anything to match Learys crazy cow. Send out for lunch. County pays. Last of the food eaten. Coke drunk. Get up and stretch. Well, time we be gettin back. Look solemn. Damn near laughed looking at ol Big Jim sittin there. Yes we have your Honor (oh, you bet we have, long before we ever got on this here jury). No jumping up and cheering when verdict read. Still 12 solemn faces, as others cheer and pound Big Jim, with insides singing and cheering and laughing, damn, its good to be alive. Aint no body showin us how to live and thats for damn sure. No, no one can show them how to live. Certainly not how to think. Cokcola and bourbon. Where does a person like that come from? How does an entire population make him a hero? God, this is disgusting. This is beyond anything… Yeah, even Barnard. Well…maybe not? Maybe he was more insidious. No one will ever know how many men, and women, died because he was 'just doing his job'. No one will ever know. At least Big Jim did do it personally. Hands on as the saying goes. He didnt hide behind a desk and a bureaucracy. Have to give him that. Still no justification. They both destroyed innocent lives…no justification. Cant always avoid justice indefinitely. Evil can not be allowed to exist and grow…especially when it has been uncovered. No, absolutely not. To allow that…to permit evil to continue is to be a part of it…to encourage it. Must learn the lesson of Nuremberg. Where does he come from? What does he do? How does he live with this???? Mr Kinsey, Big Jim, you good ol boy, bet yuall never did hear of the Internet. Well, dont make no never minds, cause it be tellin me all about you. Oh yes sir, Big Jim, it be tellin me the size of your shoes, the color of your eyes, the brand of your underwear, and if you ever wash them. Oh, Mr Kinsey sir, I can sit right here in the comfort of my yankee home and know more about you than you know about yourself…well, that doesnt mean much, does it, considering you probably have no idea what you are and what you are about…just like the rest of your ilk. Well, I/ll tell you something you will never know, self-deception is only that. It is only the self that is deceived. I will not be deceived…or stay as ignorant of you as you are. You are a disgusting bug and bugs can be eliminated and not allowed to befoul the air the rest of us breathe, or the ground we walk upon. You and your ignorance have wreaked enough havoc on the rest of us, oh god, they vote, all the Big Jims and good ol boys vote…no wonder there are so many Jesse Helmses in Congress, and we pay the price of their ignorant viciousness…

Is it not written that you will not be left comfortless? The man is so absorbed in his new task he is unaware how completely he has surrendered to it. Unaware, too, that he knows not where the gun is, the gun that was so much a part of him for 2 days he could not tell where he ended and the gun began. For many endless hours he sat on the couch with the barrel of the gun in his mouth, hoping to bring his tragic and painful life to an end, wanting nothing more than to leave this nothingness for a permanent and eternal nothingness, yet, once again, in the wink of an eye he has cast off the shroud of that nothingness without even being aware of it, without having planned to do so. Has this not happened before? Many times?

In his cokcola, how wonderfully fitting and poetic to perform this little ceremony on the day of the picnic, the towns celebration of putting the niggas in their place… Could just cover all those fine ribs with it, let them all have a *taste* of it. No, cant do that. Cant kill innocent people INNOCENT!!!! Innocent???? Yeah, there are… I guess. Certainly the kids. And some of the younger people. Probably have no idea what its all about. But most of them deserve dying as much as Big Jim. At least the jury. Can get their names in a minute. Probably still alive, just like him. Those kind never die…they dont even fade away. Why? Why in the name of hell do they thrive so much? Nothing ever seems to bother them. Live forever and it never rains on their parade. Well, its going to rain on their picnic. Oh yeah, this is one time the heavens will piss all over those bastards. A massive case of food poisoning. Have to be careful, no kids. Have a whole year to prepare, to plan, to get things ready. Hmmm, a whole year. Seems like a long time to wait. They should be dispatched with extreme prejudice right now! Prudence. Best be cautious. Haste and waste and all that sort of thing. There are some serious logistical problems that need to be solved. Not as simple as Barnard. Crowded coffee shop, no body noticing you. Different situation. A little hick town. They sure as hell will notice a stranger, especially on Freedom Day. But they are used to reporters being there at their picnic. Could go unnoticed. But suppose they get a shot of me on the television. Might cause a problem. Haste and waste. Relax. Dont need to solve all the problems now. Just relax… Yeah, he cant stay in that hick town all the time. Must need to go to other places. Yeah…if I cant get him on his home turf maybe I can get him on the road…

Hmmmm…now thats an interesting idea… Need to give this some serious thought. Those reporters certainly knew a lot about ol Big Jim, the networks have all that info in their libraries…yeah…but cant go to them, too obvious and incriminating. What the hell did Big Jim say??? there was something that made me think…shit, what the hell was it???? Seems like something inside of me noticed something about it…damn what in the hell was it??? nothing really extraordinary, just kind of *en passant*, but there was a click inside. Krist, this is aggravating. Damn, too bad I didnt tape it, no, no, better not to remember than to have something like that in the house. Even if it is just a video image, things that disgusting should not be in the house, ol Big Jim Kinsey. The souths gift to humanity. Loathsome, despicable son of, hell what was it? Drive myself goofy if I sit here trying to remember. Bes be taking a stroll down by the town square surenuf thank you mam an all the good ol stuff. Balls. Cant remember it and cant stop trying…maybe I should go for a walk. Some pie and coffee might help, an maybe a little people watching or newspaper or something. Yeah, sounds good to me…

Delightful night. Refreshing…really refreshing. Jacket feels good, damn, dont even remember thinking to put it on. Wonder how I figured that one out? Guess Im just a genius. Who woulda thought? Cool air feels wonderful. Had no idea how hot I was, at least my head…or should I say, my fevered brow? Yeah, think I will. Guess thats where that expression 'He makes my blood boil' comes from. Wonder what the boiling temperature of blood is?

Boy, the sparrows are really chirping up a storm. Guess theyre feeling invigorated by the air. Wonder what it would be like if they replaced car horns with sparrow chirps? Pretty funny. Have to get one up and replace it with a blue jay squawk or crow caw or…oh god, that/d killya, a peacock screech. Whoa, think I/d rather have the good old fashioned car horn…

Well, well, still some diners, if thats the right word for people eating in a deli. Sounds better than eaters. Whose eating whom? Oh well, blueberry pie and vanilla ice cream can change anyones perception and bring a lightness to the mind and heart. Really dont like to be gauche, but have to eat it with a spoon. A fork just doesnt cut it, so to speak. Theres always that final blend of melted ice cream and blueberry filling. Oh god, if only it were possible to live on this. Oh, tis a consummation dev—Ah just dont care what all those people are always sayin bout me. Thats it! Right! Thats what he said. Oh thank god Ive finished the pie and ice cream. If I hadnt I might have to leave some behind as I rush home. What a wonder the mind is. Waited until I finished eating before giving me the answer. Oh how sweet the caring charms of Providence. To home, home…home where the heart is…and the Internet. But wait a non sweet Horatio. Leave us take our time. All is in perfect order and will be when we log on. Is it not sweet dear Prince to tantalize one self for a few precious moments? Yes, yes indeed. Stroll past the trees lined with chirping birds and the parked cars dotted with their drippings…or is it droppings? Looks like polka dots and moonbeams. Pretty tune but a lousy metaphor. When its your car its just plain bird shit. Thank god dogs cant fly. Now that would really be a revolting development…

So, home where the heart is…and the Internet… Clickity clack, clackity click… Yeah, go for it…okay, I/ll try it…and one more…and, Wow! A picture and all oh, more than one… I see, some old ones. From the trial. Sure has put on some weight. Good eatin and an untroubled conscience. Do it every time. God, theres more info on this guy than Babe Ruth. Damn near a daily diary since the trial…hmmm, really gets heavy after the first Liberation Day Barbecue. They say you should know your enemy, but this…

Only need the more recent stuff…what are his habits today? Where do you go Mr Big Jim Kinsey? Do you bowl, go to ball games, some place, some place…no, that bars too small, probably same faces day after day, year after year…same diner…same store…down the road a few miles…no, no…need to find some place where he/ll go where I can get lost in the crowd and I/ll know definitely ahead of time when he will be there. In and out. No over night in a motel. Hello, goodbye. Yeah, bye, bye baby. Something big. Lots of people. Something he always goes to. Crowds to get lost in. Oh Jimmy, Jimmy, you caint stay holed up in the piss ant town all the time. You must go somewheres with people. You must go somewhere… Relax…relax. Plenty of time. Been browsing a couple of hours. Tons to digest. Youll find it. Its there, somewhere. Youll find it. Tomorrow…next day…whenever. No rush. Long day. Yeah, really long day. Stretch…walk around in circles for a few minutes…unlax then go to bed. Gone through a lot of changes today. Jesus, sure as hell have. Forgot. Most of the day like last few days. That lousy gun in my mouth. Feeling so bad I couldnt kill myself. Jesus, just a few hours ago. That eye is winking again. Emotionally wasted. But a bit hyped too. Just like that. Wink, wink. Looking forward to tomorrow. Theres always hope…always something to live for. If you can just hang in until you find it. Yeah. Thank god Ive found it. Again. Ye old winking eye. Well, while its winking these are going to shut. Beat. Will sleep the deep sleep of an untroubled conscience. So Big Jim, you good ol boy, we have something in common. Ha, ha, yeah, if I really believed that I would kill myself. Ahhh, but I havent and so youll meet your demise. Oh Big Jim, your days are numbered and limited. Yeah…numbered and as limited as your intelligence…you fat bigoted slob. An lets see how many jurors are still around. They truly are your peers and you undoubtedly deserve each other, hey wait a minute… I never noticed that or gave it a thought. All that talk about 30 years ago and I didnt do the arithmetic. You were just a young fella then, werent you Jimbo? Somewhere in your early twenties. Too old to be on a vision quest, to pass through the rites of manhood, but maybe thats what you were doing? Trying to prove something. Not too bright, got out of high school and went to work in the chicken packing plant. High school career 'undistinguished'. Academically the bottom of the class; Socially, bottom of the barrel; Athletically, not even a runner-up in beer drinking. So Big Jim, you were a big zero, a nothing, lonely, lost, a poor little lamb who has gone astray. Damn, you werent even a good car mechanic. Just putter around in a beat up pickup truck. Certainly didnt have a date for the prom, if they had a prom. Stayed home and squeezed your pimples. Yeah, a lousy deal Jim. When youre invisible in a town the size of yours you are truly the invisible man. But youre not invisible anymore. Youre somebody now. Admired. Respected. An annual barbecue in your honor. Yes indeedy do. And all you had to do was murder a couple of black doctors. Damn, I wonder when you go to the big barbecue in the sky if those doctors will be waiting for you? Something to consider I would say. Suppose you have to pass a physical? A complete physical, enemas, probes, the whole works. My, my, my, wonder if one of them was a proctologist. Oh Big Jim, I think youd better opt for hell, it will be much more to your liking. Anyway, enough of this for now. Need to get to bed and rest these tired bones and weary eyes. My god, last night I went to bed with the taste of gun metal in my mouth and tonight I worked until my eyes started closing and Im looking forward to getting up tomorrow morning and getting back to work. I really feel like theres a valid reason to be alive, something to look forward to.

Yes, is it not wondrous what changes can occur in the wink of an eye? Does not everyone need a reason to live? To make worthwhile the effort of staying alive through such arduous trials, the unreasonable demands made by life upon human frailty? Indeed, such is always the case. And has he not done so exceptional a job of enduring the labors forced upon him? Look...look how soundly and innocently he sleeps. How well he encompasses the combination of human frailty and endurance. Even in the depths of his despair I had faith in him. Has he not always prevailed over these self-same trials and tribulations? It is of no matter when I look into him I find no fault. Vengeance is the Lords, but retribution is in the hands, and hearts, of the righteous. Sleep well. Rest well your stout heart and innocent mind faultless warrior.

...my god, there must be hundreds, thousands of people adding information to this website. No idea this guy even existed, but obviously a lot of people do. Why hasnt someone killed him? Guess they dont know how to do it without getting caught. Im sure Im not the only one who wouldnt want to go to prison for killing vermin like that. He looks like a stuffed pig and he/ll die like one. Wonder if someone will tape it. Great end to his website. Yeah, happy ending nice and tidy. But how can I E.coli him and the jury? Will probably have to be done all in the same day. Cant make more than one trip...too dangerous. Lots of shots of the jury after the trial, but what about now? Lets see how many are still alive...couple of them looked old enough at the trial to be dead now. Thirty years is thirty years. Big ol Jim could have another thirty in him...yeah, thats right Jimbo, they may be in you but you aint gonna live them out, and thats for damn sure, Im— Wow, look at that. A group shot at the first barbecue...yeah, they do, one for every year. Man, these people are quick, even got this years already. Yeah, thought so, only eleven. Looks like ol Bubba died just a few months ago… I didnt even know he was sick. Dont know when JR died. Hope it was painful. Two less to consider. They all get food poisoning, and no one else, going to look suspicious. Dont have to be a Sherlock Holmes to see something fluky about that… Yeah…thats true…whats the difference? They can have all the suspicions they want, autopsy all they want…even believe what they want. What do they end up with? Eleven people dead from food poisoning. So it cant be coincidence, so what? No problem…just not a problem. Can even add a little spice to the project. A just ending to this website. Oh no, no way, thats one temptation I will not indulge. Im not adding one word. Will be fun to see what people have to say when they all go belly up. Enough, enough fantasy, have to get back to downloading the pictures and finding some way to get the culture into them…and only them. Well, maybe Big Jims good ol boy who kept putting his big ol han in front of the camra. We/ll see how that works out. Sure hes pic—yeah, there he is, Clyde. Yeah, an even dozen. Good photos. No trouble recognizing them…damn, Im dizzy. Krist, I havent eaten today. Better nuke something. Whatever I grab. Can still get in a couple more hours of work.

…have to keep all this stuff neat. All good stuff…good photos. Somebody put quality stuff on the web. By the time I get to wherever Im going to go I/ll recognize these guys in the dark with their backs turned to me. Yeah, where am I going to go? Who knows. I/ll recognize it when I come across it. Must be some place other than the barbecue where they all get together…some place public…accessible. Somewhere in all this information is the place. Some place where a stranger wouldnt be noticed. Just an anonymous face among many. No connection to Big Jim. A nothing before the trial, a nothing since, only now hes a well-known nothing. Likes Marlboro cigarettes, coffee, beer, rutabagas, biscuits and gravy, ribs, grits, etc., etc… Well, I have plenty of time. I also have a bundle of information. Eyes are closing. Krist, no wonder, its late. Thats the trouble with stopping for a minute, realize youre exhausted. Another day. Incredible. Those other days were an eternity, these last 2 have gone by in the wink of an eye. These eyes aint winking. God, look at that pile of paper. No wonder my eyes are closing. Ive gone through a bundle of stuff. Oh thats great. Really been productive. Tomorrows another day. Another day closer to Big Jims demise. Yeah. Thats it! Ol Big Jim Kinsey has given me a reason to live. I/ll never have to suck on the barrel of a gun again. My life is not meaningless, purposeless. Youth springs eternally in my mind and heart. How about you Jimbo? What springs in your heart and mind? God, I/d love to know. Do you even have a heart? I know you have a mind, one that is corrupt and contaminated, like a cess pool. A terrible place to be. Maybe Quayle was thinking of you Jimbo…a mind is a terrible thing. Especially when it is allowed to go unattended. Was there ever an attempt to tend yours? Did you get your heart broken when you was a youngun and that poisoned your unattended mind? Did the kids poke fun at the hole in your britches? Did they tease you because of your cowlick? What manner of abuse desiccated your heart and defiled your mind? Or is it genetic? Does ignorance and bigotry become genetic after so many generations? Are you a product of your environment, your family, of States Rights? Perhaps youre just a rotten son of a bitch and would always be a rotten son of a bitch no matter what mommy and daddy did or didnt do. Achhh, cant let myself get caught up in this and allow his disease to infect me. Dont need to carry this garbage to sleep with me. Imperative I remain detached, objective, no emotional involvement one way or the other. Right, no more so than a surgeon about to amputate an infected limb that is endangering a persons life. Must remain detached to be effective. No, youre not going to infect me James Kinsey. I am going to stretch out on my bed and allow myself to ease into a restful and refreshing sleep and awake in the morning with the gentle sunlight coming through the shades and curtains and joyously greet the new day and smile and sing as I get up, take a leak, shower, shave, dress, and continue to discover more about the Jim Kinsey of the past so I can, as rapidly as possible, guarantee he has no future.

The man moves me. His sentiments are so heartfelt, are they not? It is not just that he is without fault. No. It is now his virtue that shines forth so brilliantly...as does his awareness.

...forgot about food again. Better nuke something and get back to work. Good idea to take a few minutes off and think about this, what am I eating??? Hmmm, Meatless Lasagna. What do you know? Thought it was a turkey dinner. Need to think about this. Ton of info on those guys—damn, cant get used to two being women. Wonder why? Strange. Guess they did let women on the juries, at least white women. Didnt realize Joey was Josephine, and Les was Leslie. Cant really tell from the old jury pictures. Sort of fuzzy. Wasnt looking for women. Oh well, no big deal. Two are women. Got 10 lb dossiers on all of them. Doesnt really help. Cant find the Lowest Common Denominator. No point in still hunting. Maybe cant get them all at one time. Yeah, might be that way. Well, we/ll see what Providence has in mind. Getting them all at once can be a stretch. Who knows what opportunity may present itself... Of course they will have to be addressed too. Fact that theyre women doesnt change that. They all share in the responsibility. Matter of Equal Rights. Womens Lib proved that. Wouldnt want to have a discrimination suit filed against me by NOW. No indeed. Can they file one against an 'anonymous' person? How would they do that? Jane Doe/John Doe? To Whom it May Concern? Wonder how the courts will deal with that? Interesting legal question. Theyre both mothers...and the men are fathers, least 8 of them are. Funny how thats supposed to make a difference. If youve given birth to a child your responsibility diminishes. Crazy. Culpable is culpable. Have to decide, now, if I should continue—no, no. No more checking these people. I/ll go nuts. Focus on Big Jim. Must be common place. He/ll show me the way. Where would they all go where I wouldnt be noticed? If I turned myself into a woodpecker I/d be noticed in that town. Must be someplace in the area...like a cokcola bottling plant, that would be big doings...a horse race, pig race, some damn thing—yeah, pig race. County Fair. Wouldnt they all go to a County Fair? Must. What the hell else is there to look forward to? Easter egg hunt? Probably all go together. Sure. Same bus. Have a good ol time. I guess. Wouldnt they show up sooner or later? Dont have to get them all the same day. Would a belly full of beer kill the bugs? Dont think so. Can check that out. County Fair. Sounds good. Probably at the County Seat. Think thats how it usually works. Can check all that out easy enough. Just make sure I have plenty of culture. Yeah, a lot of it, they need all the culture they can get. Might civilize those yahoos. Always said lack of culture was their problem—Whoa, whoa, whoa, whats this, Leslie Snopes wins third place in sharpshooting at the County Fair Gun Show! Of course, thats where theyll all congregate. They aint no stinkin farmers. No, but they sure are a bunch of pigs. Sure looks happy. Big ass grin. Gun looks like a part of her. Oh, wait a minute, NOW should check this out. She got the medal for 3rd place in the 'Womens Division' even though she got a higher score than the 3rd place man. Think I/ll call the Equal Rights Commission. This is blatant sexism. I am aghast, flabbergasted to see that there is sexism in the sunny south. Guess they forgot how to keep them barefoot and pregnant. Wonder how ol Big Jim feels about this. Dont see him congratulating her. Matter of fact dont see any men. Couple of kids...hmmm, grandchildren. Guess its tolerable. Its not like she can chop a tree down faster, or change a tire faster, or rebuild an old Chevy faster, or drink beer faster. Thats still the inviolable province of men...real men. And, of course, murderin niggas. Big Jim may not even know her, so to speak. Just a nodding acquaintance on the street. Seems like the women never had anything to do with lynching and other forms of murder. Maybe just agitate...provoke. Power behind the scene. No, they dont need anyone pushing them into it. Sure Big Jim wasnt willing to let the Black Doctors go their way until some woman threatened his manhood and shamed him into it. As a matter of fact theres nary a mention of Ol Jimbo and a woman. Friends say he is a 'sportin man' so I guess he does get laid from time to time, but never no girlfriend, not even in high school. Sunday school? Maybe the lamb in the manger. Careful Jimbo, dont want to make your favorite goat jealous. Those kids sure look proud of their Grandma. Oh well, why not? She won something. I suppose she loves her grandchildren as much as any grandmother. They say Hitler loved his dog. Im sure all those people who spent their working day participating in some way in the death of those millions of people love their kids. Ahhh, this is all bullshit. Let the philosophers worry about all that. Evil is evil, period. Just because a man loves his children doesnt mean he should be allowed to murder whomever he chooses. There comes a time when we must say no to the tyranny of ignorance and do whatever is needed to bring about its demise. Jefferson and the other Founding Fathers knew that all too well. Oh god, Im tired. Eyes feel like two piss holes in a snow bank. Enough of this mental masturbation. County Fair is the place. Think they usually happen around September, check it out tomorrow. Feel dizzy. To bed, to bed…to bed and sleep, to sleep perchance to dream. Aye, theres the rub, for in that dream of Big Jims death what peace will come? A whole bunch I would say. Yeah, yuall bet yo cotton pickin ass. Goodnight Mrs Calabash, wherever you are.

The more he pursues his quarry the more jovial and playful does he become. It would appear there is more than the winking of an eye operating here.

…really have no choice, they were just as eager as the men to let Big Jim off, and have been participating in the celebration every year. Shit, not only participating but contributing, eagerly. '…thas raight, me an Les been bakin paies an crullers an batches a fritters…ol Jim jus loves his corn fritters…ah sometimes figure he thinkin about them corn fritters all the year, we doan givem none no other time…' Damn, you can hear them giggling and laughing just reading this. You can actually *see* how proud they are of what theyve done and are doing. Not only no apology or questioning their actions, but absolute pride. No, I cant allow myself to get caught up in this 'preferential treatment' for women. They are all equally guilty. Just have to dismiss all qualms about the women. They have been arguing for equal pay for equal work for years and I will most assuredly abide by that request…oh yes indeedy do. We sho enuf bake our big fat asses off, sho nuf, sho nuf. Corn fritters!!!! Oh…is it possible? Die from eating corn fritters? Oh dear god in heaven, let me find a way to dispatch, with extreme prejudice, Big Jim with corn fritters. Please Lord, please…pretty please with sugar on it. I/ll make a novena, say a hundred Hail Marys and a fistful of Our Fathers. I/ll even make already a pilgrimage to the Bronx (god bless the mark). Whoa now, easy does it. Dont let personal pride and satisfaction get in the way of our responsibility. The important thing is to free the world of that vermin, thats number one. Must remember, first things first. Then comes the jury. And certainly do not want to end up in prison for it so must be simple food poisoning. To do it at the 'barbecue' is taking an unnecessary risk, the exposure would be dangerous. Thats where they have the corn fritters. Would probably have them at the Fair, but dont know if possible there. It would be like a lifetime of Christmases and Birthdays, but cant jeopardize myself for the ego satisfaction. However…wouldnt it be wonderful? No, no, drop it. Krist, as it is its not all that easy. Getting enough culture into Big Jim, and the jury, is going to take some work. Certainly dont know ahead of time about the effectiveness of the culture, always the possibility that it wont be effective. Have some that I know is lethal, and have ample time to let that grow…say in unpasteurized apple juice. Should make it easy to dispense. Have to be careful, very careful. May just as well get this all straight in my head now. Easiest way to dispense it is in the ever present cokcola. Need to bring a large amount to be certain. Have time to get more information, but seems like will need a large dose of very virulent culture in case theyre drinking a lot of beer. The alcohol may destroy at least some of the culture. Still a lot of work to be done. Plenty of time, no rush. Maybe I should check out some other fairs first to familiarize myself. Not a good idea. Get accustomed to one layout and if the other is different it may cause confusion. No, have to keep it simple. Plan but not project. Need to remember to live in the now and respond to the moment. No good to stay locked in a plan. Must keep flexible. No way of knowing what I will encounter. I/ll know what to do when it is time to do it. For now, let it all go. Need to take better care of myself. No need to get so immersed in work I forget to eat. I have time. A couple of months before the County Fair opens. More than ample time to do all that needs doing. Must pay close attention to details. Get each and every detail in proper order and everything will be just fine. Okay, time to give you, and me, some rest. See you in the morning.

The mans prayer moves and pleases me. I reach down and Bless him, My Light Shine upon and through him from this day forward through all eternity. He is most pleasing to my eye, deserving in my heart. Peace be yours my son.

Seems like such a long time since I turned you on. Seems like years since I ate breakfast before turning you on. Did you think I left town? Well, fear not noble friend and co-worker. Should only be a few more days of such intense work on our little project then we can get back to business as usual, at least for a while. Soon I/ll be going away for a few days, but I shall return. I feel such a power in my hands, fingers, and a peace in my heart. I am filled with an incredible lightness of being as if I am part of the air I breathe—enough, enough of such whimsy and ethereal thoughts. To work. There are serious deeds to perform, and much preparation needed to perform them. Yes, yes, by all means, we will start with the days of the Fair. The love potion has already been mixed and even now foments its message of love knowing full well that I will deliver it. Oh yes, I will deliver it you assless, potbellied boil on the armpit of life. You will know how much you are loved. And the other ten prime examples of human dignity. For love has truly pitched its tent in the place of excrement (sorry about that WBY). Now for the method of delivery. Cokcola best. But will stay open to all necessity…however it may present itself. Some foods are always a possibility: beans, chili, barbecue… Getting it on the food undetected. Looks like youve given me all the help you can for now. Thank you kindly mam. Hmmm…I guess so. Just like a ship is 'she'. Theyre such workhorses, yet theyre called 'she'. Well, they do have beautiful lines. Is that why theyre called she? Somehow dont think so. Check that out sometime. Are a lifeline. So are you sweetheart. A line to anyplace, anywhere. Certainly a line to the heart of the matter we/re concerned with. Okay, I/ll give you a rest and all this a little thought.

…yeah,

thats true, doesnt all have to happen in one day. Lasts a week. Theyll be there couple of days. Suppose it doesnt kill them? Always a possibility. A very distinct possibility.

Have to accept that. Didnt know if it would work with Barnard. This is not a one shot deal. Can always try again, and again. Do whatever is necessary. Certain things are *a priori* in a situation like this. Not going to test the culture on some poor, innocent little creature. Killing vermin like Big Jim is one thing, but a pussy cat…that would be an abomination. Enough of this meaningless speculation. Went through all this with Barnard. This is so much more complicated…and dangerous. Lets see, whats needed? First: A safe, fool proof way to transport the culture. Second: Safe, fool proof way to 'deliver' it… I think thats the phrase. Vials, stoppers and wax should keep it safe. Just like canning food. Do it right, dont want botulism. Can make you sick, even kill you. Krist, have to stop this nonsense. No time for stupid jokes. Seal them and pack them in styrofoam. Thats no problem. Its at the Fair…need to think this through… Wait! No more circles. What worked with Barnard will work with anyone. No more agonizing over this. Finished. Over. Just get to culturing whats needed. Have to remember, first things first. Stop shaving. No haircut. Should look just like everyone else when I get there. God thats a terrible thought. However… Disappear in the crowd. Give my brain a rest until then.

Hi.

Hi.

How long you fixin to stay?

Not sure exactly.

You here for the Fair?

Fair?

The County Fair.

Oh. Maybe so. See how it works out. Ahh, which way is it from here?

Just go down 37 a ways, an past the Mobil Station youll see a fork. Take the left. Plenty a signs. Only couple a miles.

Thanks. Just might do that.

Nice enough room. Can actually turn around. Stretch out for a little while, then see what the Fair is like. Should I carry all the bottles? Seems strange. A dozen. Nobodys going to see them. No one is going to check my inside pockets in my jacket. Have to stop feeling self-conscious. It always attracts attention. Have to always be prepared. The perfect opportunity may be there and if I dont have enough…right. They all come with me. Tested them a hundred times, never leaked a drop. No problem. I/ll bring a dozen.

Damn, only a few cars in the parking lot…and a thousand pickup trucks… Well, here goes. Just walk around and let Providence guide me. If the Red Sea can be parted I should be able to find a couple of good ol boys in this crowd… Hmmm, that food smells good. Time to eat… Guess I/ll park myself here and look around while I eat. Everybody looks so similar. Didnt think I/d have this problem. Dont want to make a mistake. This is not an act of terrorism but retribution. Vengeance may be the

Lords, but Im going to give him a little help. I/ll just drift through the crowd and…hmmm, skeet shooting contest tomorrow…might be a good idea if I checked out the area so I—Oops, ahm sorry, hope I didnt (my God! Its Les) get anythin on yuall.

Oh, ah, no, not at all.

Must be gettin clumsy in my old age. Here, let me put this tray down an clean up this dress, just put it on clean this mornin an look at it, now aint that a sight (got to get a bottle out…she really looks like a grandmother). Would you keep a eye on this tray while I get some more napkins?

Oh…certainly, yeah. (Just move it over and…over. Simple. Done.)

A little cold water should take care of it. Should dry up jus fine.

I would think so—

Now what chuall doin Les, flirtin with this here young man?

Now you be hushin your mouth Clyde an that means no laughin too.

Can I put down this tray and join yuall anyway?

Dont this jus beat all, clean an crisp when I left the house an—

Hey, youre not leavin?

Sorry, have to meet someone. Dont want to be late.

Well, I sure know what you mean.

Now Clyde, you stop that school boy grinnin and laughin an let the man be. Dont pay him no mind.

Ahh, nice meeting you…all.

Oh god, have

to walk straight, not too fast, easy does it. No panic. Just keep smiling and moving toward the parking lot. Have to get to the car. Just one step at a time. Move one foot then the other. Breathe, breathe. Doesnt make any difference how, just breathe. Never mind slow and deep. Fuck the panic, just keep breathing and moving. Every step and every breath the car is closer, and closer. Dont run? Krist, I couldnt if I tried. Oh shit, wheres the car? I know, I know, D-7. No need to panic, just move and breathe, move and breathe. God that sun is hot. Not too bad under those canopies, but out here…my throat is actually dry and raspy. Where the hells the car, it should be right there… yeah, right, behind the pickup truck. Cant see it from here. Oh thank god, there it is. Few more feet. Jesus its hot in here. Get these windows open and ac on. Whew, thats better. Just sit, catch my breath, calm down. Still too shaky to drive. Few more minutes. My head is spinning. Okay, now relax…now breathe deep and slow… yeah, relax. Got to get out of here but cant drive until Im relaxed. Deep and slow… Just be aware. Drive slowly, but not too slow, dont draw attention. Take it easy…yeah…

Oh god, never thought I/d be so grateful to be in a hick town motel. Let me get under that shower…

Oh, feels good to air dry. Still day light and I feel like Ive been wrung through a dozen wringers. Clyde and Les. Really got me off balance. But I did it. I/ll be more in control from now on. Never expected that sort of confrontation.

Almost paralyzed me. But I recovered…and got the job done… Bet if you saw Hitler with his dog you/d think what a nice man he is, really loves his dog. Mass murderers dont walk around with a sign hanging from their necks. Thats why Hester had to wear an A. This whole idea of excusing women for heinous crimes simply because theyre women is insane. Have to see if the culture works. Wonder how I/ll know? No problem with Barnard. Even if I can get to all of them how will I know? Maybe something on the web page. If anyone finds out it will be there. Yeah. More important things to think about now. First things first. Clyde surprised me more than Les. Figured he/d be some kind of bonus. Standing right there. Big grin. Nice smile. Looked normal. Cant judge by appearances. See what happens tonight. Thats okay if they recognize me. Fireworks good time. Say Big Jim loves them. We/ll see, we/ll see. Two down. Give it all a rest.

Really a festive feeling. Guess its always that way at night. Always a feeling of work during the day, even at a Fair, but night is for playing. Fireworks sure help, especially the kids, all hyped up. Yeah, not just kids, everybody loves them, but it sure is a bigger deal for the kids. Sure did love them. One of the best things about summer. Every Tuesday night…July & August it seems like. Seems like I sat on Pops shoulders when I was little…hmmm, interesting, wonder if thats a fantasy or a reality? Crazy what you remember and what you wonder. Also cooler at night. That helps. Hint of a breeze too. Wish I didnt have this beard, so nice to lean into a breeze and feel it on your face. Hopefully off soon. Wonder if I/ll run into them? Possible they wont recognize me. Dont think they really got a good look at me. Food smells better at night too. Maybe the air is heavier and the aroma doesnt dissipate. I guess everything enjoyable is better at night, even work. And I have a job to do. Ancient memories when you could hide in the shadows. Still some, but it would take a while to find them. Floodlights everywhere. Lots of kids tugging on womens arms. Wonder if mothers have an arm longer than the other by the time their kids grow up? Could be. Dont imagine anyone has given that any thought. May just as well go with the flow. They seem to know what theyre doing. Big Jim must be here somewhere. An awful lot of people. Slowly stroll…just keep concentrating. Everybody has a drink container. Wonder if its like that at all Fairs? Okay, time to stop idle speculation. Should be easy to spot. He fits his name. Ohh, they have a little grandstand. Nice for the kids. But he seems like a standing man. Good ol boy. Gladly give his seat to a youngun. Thought I/d see him by now, dont—Clyde, did he see me? Seems like he looked right at me. Better just sort of amble over this way, around the chili stand and behind the pole…just in case. Have to keep him in sight—good hes not looking this way. Probably going to hook up with Jimbo. Dont see Les, or anyone else. Wonder how shes feeling? Wonder how hes feeling? Seems to be okay. A little queasy in the stomach? Would he feel it this soon? Hmmm, not sure. Different strokes for different folks. Still no Les. Important? Wheres everyone else? Of course, probably with their families. Everyone will gravitate here. No TV cam—is that him? Sure is big…and Clydes talking with him—are they looking at me? No, no! for gods sake, dont walk away. Just keep strolling. Keep them in sight. No, theyre just looking around…probably for someone…just keep strolling…moving into the crowd…if he was 6 inches shorter I might lose him…seem to have a particular destination in mind…yeah, on the side…just as I thought, out of the way of the younguns…oh yes, youre all heart Big Jim…what…theres a couple of others…yeah, yeah, Im sure, name, name, name…no Les, but four untainted souls—whoa…have to slow down…hearts pounding, jesus krist, breathe slowly, in and out, in and out…cant screw up now…in and out, in and out…know exactly what to do…quick dump in their cokcola…just drift in that direction…okay if Clyde recognizes me…nothing happened…cant get self-conscious…wait until the fireworks start…just keep looking at the sky…keep looking up…remember, innocent, innocent…just watching the fireworks…let the crowd push a bit…yeah Wow, that was some burst, fish wiggling all over the sky and its emptied in Jimbos cup, now just dont spill it, please god, dont let him spill ju—thats it drink it down, down, yeah drink it all up like a big boy an yo—easy, easy, stay aware, three more to go, is Clyde looking at me funny? Just keep—thats it Jimbo, drink it down—Oh that is a beauty, whoa, just keeps popping…o krist, almost spilled it on his hand, got to be careful, stay aware, aware, for gods sake dont get caught up in the damn fireworks, keep your head back but watch the cups, the cups, its in their cups, theyre in their cups for krist sake dont get hysterical, in and out, in and out, nice and slow, in and out…move about…another done…jesus, cant stop sweating, feel like my hands are dripping oh god, the sweat is getting in my eyes, can barely see, suppose I got some of the culture on my hands dont want to rub it into my eyes, please god help me get this last one…just this last one god I feel like Im holding a greased pig, the goddamn sweats burning the shit out of my eyes, what the hells going on, oh, for the love of krist stop shaking, in and out, in and out, slowly, slowly, in and out…okay, next burst…oh shit, sweating so bad I cant tell if I spilled it on my hands…no, no, its in the cup…yeah…got to move, now! Move! Drift over there…easy…just drift…swear to krist I can feel Clydes eyes burning in the back of my head—dont turn, just keep moving, work your way into the crowd…mingle…mingle…get lost in the crowd…gotta catch my breath…dizzy…fucking hearts banging through my head…maybe Im going blind…feel so woozy, shit! What the fucks going on, better move, dont want to attract attention, oh fuck, too dizzy to move, just keeps pounding in my head and chest, slow down you son of a bitch, oh fuck, slow, s l o w, s l o w…okay, have to move, have to start for the parking lot, just take it nice an easy…one foot in front of the other, one little step at a time…slow and easy…want to get there before the stampede, fireworks must be about over, o krist, dont want to get caught up in that tangle of cars…pickup trucks.

Okay, almost there...few other people beating the rush, good, wont attract attention—not important, didnt do anything, no crime, no shooting or bombs, nobody knows anything happened, just like Barnard, nothing to run from, just keep putting one foot in front of the other, shit, not even Clyde knows what happened. Never will. None of them will. Just a couple a good ol boys (and gal) got some bad barbecue an damn if it didnt kill them dead, sure nuff. Yeah, good to hear the people and hear car doors slamming and soon...yeah, there it is. Always surprised. Guess Im looking for my car and not a rental. Oh, it feels good to sit. My legs are trembling for krist sake. Fine, fine. Just get on out of here and back to the motel. Whoa, the parking lot is starting to fill up with people. Get outta here. Nice and easy. Not too slow, but cautious. Good, good, traffics moving...o krist, Ive never been so happy to leave a parking lot in my life. Concentrate on driving. Careful of the creatures that come running across the road. Dont want to kill a raccoon or a deer, or whatever they have around here. No, no, the radio wont help, not that shit kicking music. Just keep breathing and staying aware and be back in the motel before I know it and can pop a nice cold can of cokcola.

Better wash my hands first...better safe than sorry... So this is the can that launched a thousand Big Jims into the world. Heres to you Jimbo, you good ol boy...oh boy, oh boy. He stuck in his thumb and pulled out a cokcola. What a night. A night to remember. Oh what a rogue and peasant slave am I. Actually, Im more pleasant than peasant. Its ever onward into the breach, dauntless, fearless, brave souls. Or should I turn on the boob tube and see whats happening?

What the hell is this? Station after station, talk, talk, talk about the devil and the liberal democrats, what??? They still looking for communists? I dont believe this shit. Give me an amen and thank you jesus...whats with these people? This whole world is one big trailer park. They hate everybody. If theyre not hanging 'gays' theyre hanging 'feminists', oh thank god for an 'off' button. Krist, my heart is pounding. Where am I? This cant be the same country I spent my entire life in. This is beyond anything I imagined. My bodys pounding. Dizzy. Jesus my head hurts. Did I eat???? Cant fucking remember, oh these ignorant bastards. God tells them its just peachy keen to kill, maim and slaughter 'them', the unbelievers, oh shit, my fucking head is killing me. Should rest, big day tomorrow. Eight more to go. Lots of guns, guns, guns. Have to practice. Cant shoot the fucking head off a faggot or a feminist or a nigga, or a catholic or a buddhist or some other cult or a jew or muslim or all of the above. If you aint usins you is doomed to hell. Gotta drop this shit. Cant let their hate poison me. Have to get ready for tomorrow. Should I wait for night? Yeah, it is easier in some ways. But easier to recognize people in the daylight. Especially people I dont know. Shit, dont want to wait for night. I dont know, I dont know... Something doesnt feel right. Have this strong urge to leave. Just go home. What the hell is that all about? Why do I want to run? Have to get the rest of them. Thats why Im here. Cant go sneaking off in the night like some fucking redneck. Its out of the question. Cant run off and let those 8 live. I have all this culture. Theres nothing to fear. Even if Clyde recog—maybe it has nothing to do with that? Suppose its what might happen? Everytime I dont listen to my gut I regret it. I follow that and Im alright. Ridiculous. Im just excited. This aint the same. Hyped from the tension. Just an adrenaline rush. Mixed with all that fundamentalist garbage. Drive you nuts. Cant stop now. Oh shit. Shit! Madness! Absolute madness!!!! Take a walk. Run up and down the highway. Anything. Fuck what people will think. Walk it off...

Long time since I walked along a road. A kid at camp. Walk against the traffic and stay to the left. Wear something white. Today you can glow in the dark. Concentrate on what Im doing. Watch for cars and stay out of their way. Simple. Maybe someone will stop and offer me a ride. Might be willing to make a u-turn and take me where I need to go. Some down home hospitality. Well, you see, I got a burst appendix and my tractor ran over my legs, but its only another 10 miles to the hospital, no need to bother yourself neighbor. Well, if you sure. How about a chaw, little tobacco helps ease the pain. Well, I thank you kindly. Dont mind if I do. Yeah, thats what I need, to chew tobacco or sniff snuff. Damn, they must be used to people walking on the road, doesnt stop them from drifting over at 80 miles an hour and seeing how close the side view mirror comes to your head. Just another redneck way to pass the time. Thats what jesus put strangers and other creatures on the road for, to fun with. Oh by crac—no. Want to calm down, not make it worse. Just keep moving and breathing deeply...

Make sure I dont turn that boob tube on. A hell of a lot more relaxed. But still have that same feeling in my gut. Quieter, but still the same. Providence, Providence... But why should I have to leave, it—Not the question. Have to go. No doubt. Message is simple and direct. Okay, thats settled. Make sure I dont leave anything here. All the cultures are safely packed, what a shame I cant use them now. Okay, we pack, pay the bill, and get going. Man, I feel so much lighter. Wow...my body is relaxed and happy. Damnedest thing. No way to figure this. Enough. Home again, home again, ditilly jig.

Wonder what the clerk meant: Aint yuall leaving kind of sudden like? Why would he ask me that? Wonder what he was really saying...thinking? Was he keeping an eye on me? Damn, is there a sheriffs car behind me...no...not that I can tell. Maybe I should start tossing the cultures out the window? No cultures no connection with anything. Ah no, cant do that. Who knows what will happen? Some dumb dog or cat or whatever else they have around here. Oh, there cant really be a problem. Have to get rid of them anyway. No need now. Silly to have them—ah, I dont know. Can never tell when they may be needed. A lot of people that need attention. But suppose they—jesus krist, relax. Return the car, get on the plane, in less than 2 hours we/re in the air, home in no time. But maybe I shouldnt have left? Might look suspicious. About what for krists sake? Nobodys been shot or strangled or whatever. Probably should have stayed and gotten the rest of them. Having to leave doesnt make any sense. Could always spend the night somewhere else and go back tomorrow. All those evil bastards going free. Oh god, this is madness, absolute madness. Always regret when I go against that intuitive sense. Providence never misleads. Jesus, open the window and get some cool night air, maybe that will stop this constant, stupid chatter. Return the car, check in at the counter, maybe get a cup of coffee and a croissant, board the plane…quietly. No more yakity yak, yak yak…

Ahhh, home truly is where the heart is. Hmm, wonder if that originally was hearth? Hearth the heart me hearties. Frig the frigate, firth the fjord, furl the topsails, stand by the Royals, cornhole the bosun, get a little drunk and you land in jaaaaaaail. Did you miss me house? Did you miss me kitchen? Easy chair? Did you miss me sweetheart? Havent been turned on for a couple of days, have you? Ooops, should watch my language. You dont turn on do you? No, no, no. Have no fear, tomorrow we will be working. No point in bothering now…and too tired. Wiped out as a matter of fact. Exhaustecated. Sun be up soon. Screw the alarm. Just wake up with the madness of a new day. Oh I missed all of you. Tomorrow we see…we see…what? Who knows? We/ll see what we see…from sea to shining sea. O krist Im beat. Goodnight Mrs Calabash…wherever you are.

The man returns, but does he return victoriously? Will he be able to become aware of the fruits of his efforts? His actions would seem to reflect that he will. In time. All things in their time.

...well, that doesnt mean anything. Less than 24 hours. Yeah, who knows if it will make the news? Possible. But that would be a while. Just keep checking the web, but no need to sit on it. Take in a movie, let the day go by, do a little work. Its in the hands of Providence.

Oh, his faith doth surely please me. Carry on, my son.

Time, time, time... Drag along, skip along, fly by, stand still, whatever you do its still the same time. 24 hours a day. Can remember, not too long ago, when time was immobile. Wouldnt move. Minutes were hours, days interminable. This is much better. Time is dragging, but this is much better. Aware, aware. Must be aware. Dont have to go back in the funk like the last time. No reason for it. There is always something that needs doing. Yeah, thats how I/ll pass the time. Was thinking of getting a dog and playing catch with him in the backyard. Or go to a park and play Frisbee. Now thats exciting. I can start the next project now, or at least develop it. Right on, everybody needs to have something 'in development', so why not your friendly little E.coli man? Yeah...that was the mistake I made last time, thinking Barnard was the only one, the alpha and omega of my work. Ho, ho, this is marvelous. Damn, simple and obvious. How come I didnt see this before? Tunnel vision. Thats why, tunnel vision. Oh wow, of course, thats it...I was too emotionally involved. I made it personal. How did I miss that? So obvious. Surgeon doesnt operate on his own children. No objectivity. Oh man, this is so great. Krist, had no idea how tense I was, how...apprehensive. Dont have to spend my life checking to see about ol Jimbo. Just go about my business, spend some time seeing whats going on in the world, take—whoa...slow down man. Get hyped and youll be out of your gourd. Okay...in...out...in...out...nice and easy...easy does it. Just, let it all go. Yeah...

Wonder upon wonder. The man is not only without fault, he is with virtue. His nobility brightens the night sky. Oh my son, my son, what joy you awaken in me and thus the world.

...what the hell is it? Seems theres been something just barely popping up the last couple of days, but cant really get a finger on it. Seems like theres a quick flash every now and then as I browse the news, but it disappears. Well, I/ll never find it thinking about it. If Providence wants me to know something its going to have to make it clearer. Oh well, only thing to do is ignore it. Dont think about it and dont look for it. Only thing that works...what time is it? Hmmm, didnt think it was so late. Maybe I/ll walk down to the deli and get a little dinner. Brisket isnt too bad. Stretch my legs. Havent been getting much exercise lately. Too wrapped up in work. Well, time for strength and health. A little one tenth of a K walk. Hey, dont forget the one tenth back. Thats not chopped liver. Walk to the deli often enough and I/ll be a regular Schwartzenberger. Now that Ive thought of it Im getting hungrier by the minute. Okay, as they say in Bellevue, Im off. See you later sweetheart.

Oh, theres the red-headed waitress. She sure is a delight, especially when she bends over the table. Now that is the kind of distraction I can really enjoy. Hmmm, white fish is one of the specials today. Little fish might be just right. Brain food. Too bad Big Jim wasnt eating fish. Catfish I guess. Dont remember if fish E.coli. Oh well, moot now. Wonder if Im going to have to go back there? Depends I guess. Wish I knew what wouldve happened if I/d stayed. In solitaire you can always peek to see what wouldve happened if you had done this instead of that. Cant here. I—

Ready to order?

Hows the white fish?

Very good. Had some myself. Tender and flaky.

Sounds good. Salad. Thousand island.

You got it.

Funny, flaky is a put-down in one case, a compliment in another. Jimbo was flaky and so was his catfish. Was I flaky in leaving? Cant peek and find out. Might have gotten a few more…maybe all of them. Theres always tomorrow. The message was too strong. Be an absolute fool to go against it. Never know why. Dont need to. Know that its always right. Im here, now, no problems. Thats good. Who knows what will happen. The—

Here you are, white fish and a salad, thousand island. Enjoy.

Thanks… Oh, now that sure does look delicious. What a beautiful stride…yeah, like 'jello on springs'. Flaky certainly doesnt apply to her. Hmmm, the fish is flaky and tasty. Feast my sense of taste and sight. Now thats pretty good for one meal.

Well,

lets see whats going on…whos killing who, or is it whom? No, its for whom the bell tolls. Well, good to know theyre still killing each other all over the world for no really good reason. Seems like most of them are trying to prove their god is bigger and better than some other god. Goofy…just plain goofy. Like kids in the school yard: my brother can kick your brothers ass! Oh yeah, well my father can kick your fathers ass. I guess nobody grows up. The world is one big playground and everyone is duking it out. Kill for the love of killing…kill for the love of Kali… Wonder what theyre doing now that they cant kill a commie for krist? Really feel for those poor christians. Of course they do have the faggots and feminists to kill for krist. Yeah…but thats not so fashionable, and certainly not pc. Guess the important thing for them is that they have some body to hate and to kill. Was so much easier when they could direct it all toward the commies. Spreading it out amongst so many people takes much more work. Ahh for the good ol days. Guess theyll pick up their assaults on Islam. Can be fashio—Oh no…no. I dont believe it. Holy jumping bald headed codfish. Wait a second, dont go jumping…but it says definitely…not 'its reported', but a very simple, definite statement. Easy does it man, it might be a mistake—Oh god, dont let this be a mistake, let it be true, totally and absolutely true…please. I/ll say a whole bunch of Hail Marys and Our Fathers. I/ll beat my chest and *mea fuckin culpa*, I/ll join the Jews for Krist and make a novena, make a novena…so whats wrong already with a little folk dancing? Oh god is good, god is really good…a regular goody two shoes. 'Oh I am glad youre dead you rascal you, I am glad youre dead you rascal you'… Okay, from the top. E.COLI OUTBREAK FELLS FOUR AT FAIR. Yippee i yay and all that good cowboy shit. Fells Four. Dont you just love that shit? Yeah…Fells Four. No one would listen to me…and others. Beef is not healthy. You just shouldnt eat it. Even if you do eat things with faces, you shouldnt eat beef. Now havent I told you that many times? Comeon, fess up, Ive told you a whole bunch of finger lickin times yuall just shouldnt be eating those ribs. Didnt I now? Dont deny it. Jus before you climbed up into your pickup truck I told you not to be eating any a those ribs. Just look at what happened to the world when Adam give up a rib. Uh uh, heap bad medicine. But you wouldnt listen, would you? No, you had to have your way, just like always, I beg, I plead, I pray but you still do just as you damn well please. Well, look wheres it got you now. Is you lookin mutha fucka? Is you lookin? Spect yuall not seein much about now. As they say in 7-card stud, 'down and dirty'. Well, not yet. Guess it will be a while before they give you a dirt blanket. But it wont be long. No siree bob, it wont be long. Four…four felled. Oh, those food concessions are catching some heat. Theyll be checkin out those butcher shops and supply houses. Yeah, theyll have good ol government agents crawling up their asses. Good. You deserve to have to crawl up those shit kicking asses. Innocent people hurt? You kidding me? Those people starve millions...millions for their goddamn beef. Eighty (80) people can live on what it takes to produce just one (1) pound of beef. The more they shut down the better— Yeah, a fringe benefit I never anticipated. A little something extra. Not of the import of the main objective, but at the same time a noble addition. Oh, I cant believe it. ALL FOUR!!!! Right the fuck on!!!! The way to go! Thats right, they havent. No mention of the murders and trial and barbecue and all that good ol boy stuff. Havent made the connection yet. Wonder what will happen when they do? Has to be a ton of suspicion. But the pm's will prove food poisoning...period. Just a weird coincidence. Guess its just as well I left. Eight more would have been something else. My god, they really would have gone apeshit. Theyll be scratching their heads and asses as it is, but 8 more??? Whoa, that would have been absolute madness. Wonder if it could have caused me any problems? Who knows, but not going to worry about that. Oh I feel good. Seems like this is better than Barnard. But that was truly a reason to rejoice. Oh man... Thank you jesus... Better start calming down. I/ll blow a blood vessel or something. Dont think Ive ever been this hyped. Holy shit. All 4 of them. Wonder if I should post something on Big Jims web page? Maybe a cryptic remark about the incident...saying nothing definite, but implying everything???? That would roast some asses. Oh that would be fun. Could even scare the shit out of the other 8. Some news wire would be sure to pick it up. Sounds good. Wouldnt do it from my own machine. Library…one of those Internet coffee shops, whatever. Oh that would be fun. I can feel the power thrusting through me. But not tonight. Just give it all time to settle in and settle down. Could send mysterious, unmarked packages to all 8 of them…or maybe just a couple…randomly. After the connections made theyll be afraid to open anything that doesnt come from Sears or Monkey Ward. Could send them a box of candy. Or a ham sandwich. A whole box of ham sandwiches. O krist, can imagine…cops and technicians all going apeshit over ham sandwiches… Hey chief, I think I found something on this one, looks really suspicious.

Yeah, its called mustard asshole.

Oh, theres a million variations. But nothing tonight. Tonight everything is cool. Just…just what? Cant sit still. Better walk it off…as much as possible anyway. Can always watch some dumbass television. That should help me sleep. Nice night for a walk, not too hot. Good idea. But just walk, no skipping and jumping up in the air and clicking my heels. And no bars and talks with bartenders. Yeah, a good walk will help. I/ll take a constitutional. Health and strength all the way.

Truly I say to you, I find no fault in this man. I rejoice and am exceedingly glad. Walk, my son, walk and feel the fresh refreshing breeze on your face. Whatever befalls you you will never be alone. Look…look now at the stars in the heavens, do they not seem brighter, if just by a little? The Blessings of the night are upon you my son. Truly I say to you you shall prosper in all your endeavors in my name.

Another day, another day. Yes indeed. And what do you have in store for me 'day'? Will you tell me now or slowly feed it to me one breath at a time. Feel a little bit like Cyrano, but giants I can do without. Now the blonde that served me this morning...now thats a whole other matter. Oh is she delectable. Such musical movements...and not like a metronome...no indeed. Really fluid, as the saying goes. Time for a song and dance ala Fred Astaire or Gene Kelly. Maybe a little 'Ive got the world on a string'...yeah, sure do feel like that, but who needs the whole world? For now one lovely blonde will do. Should really check that out. Oh well, later for that. Time to check the web page. Cant wait any longer. Tantalized myself enough. A tap a click a click a tap and......... Herrrrrrrres Jimbo!!!! Baboom. Okay, we get to the end and......yep there it is. Some people have already made the connection. Its amazing, they must spend hours every day searching for connections and posting information. But this is a little obvious. Anyway, god bless these people, wow...look at the speculations...conspiracy, conspiracy...the wrath of god, now thats a good one... Holy Mackerel! THE NIGGAS REVENGE. This is really sick... Sure have a lot of choices for responsibility: NAACP, Jackson, Farrakhan, SLC, SNCC, oh man, the list is endless. You know, this is just like the Kennedy killing: No one can believe that one little obscure misfit like Oswald could cause such a momentous event. Only in this case the event is not momentous, not in the Kennedy sense, and its something that really needed doing. But Im just me so it cant be a conspiracy. Wonder if I should suggest that on the web? No, no point. No tempting fate. No downloading info or even printing it. Just a little perusal from time to time, and never too long. Just long enough to make my little heart go pitter patter. Oh, this is so great. Its really starting to settle in…hes really dead. Big Jim Kinsey is dead and so is good ol boy Clyde. Damn! Cold stone dead in the market. Yowza, yowza, yowza, they done checked out an dont know if they has did any checkin in yet. Yeah, thats a good one, Whats your forwarding address? Paper burns and e-mail melts. Ha ha, thats good…yeah, I like that: What did you do with your sheet? Hey, maybe theyll wrap them in them? A few hundred years it may look like another shroud of Turin. That would really confuse posterity. What the hell, no reason they shouldnt be as confused as we are… Yeah, no need to try, theyll accomplish it all by themselves just as we did. E may equal MC^2, but ignorance is truly bliss. Oh man, Ive got to stop spending all my time with this web page. Fun is fun, but theres still a lot to do, much that needs accomplishing. Aint that something, dont want to close, well…there you go Jimbo. Yeah, just like that hes gone. A click of the mouse and no more Big Jim. Period. Back to browsing the news. Damn, wish I could see what in the hell is nagging at me. Something, something, something…right in front of my nose and I cant see it…yet. Shit! Better cool it.

Never see it this way and I/ll drive myself nuts. Okay, lets work for a few hours, eat dinner, and see what happens...

Maybe a little walk around the block, slowly, on the way to the deli would be a good idea. Work went well. Always does when I dont think about it. Yeah, sure, but how do you not think about a white monkey? Just have to get my head involved in something else and it will come. Yeah, speaking of which I hope the redheads working tonight. Hey, thats a good one, red, white and blue. A blonde in the morning, a redhead in the evening, and Im blue...oh, am I blue over you. Perhaps thats the distraction I need. Best one at a time though. Want to do a thorough job. Always aim to please. Concentration, thats the key. Keep them coming back. But not too often, no need for greed. Just doing what I can to keep the old red, white and blue flying. Perhaps a soft landing is even better. Oh, Im sure they are soft...and cuddly. Thats important—ah, she is here. No wonder Im not all there, just look at the music. Better not sit at one of her tables, cant trust myself. Better to worship from afar than never to have worshipped at all.

Can I help you?

I hope so sweetheart, you see—

Can I get you something to eat?

Oh...yes. I/ll have the brisket and a salad.

What kind of dressing would you like on your salad?

Italian.

You got it.

Ah, so I have... But isnt that always the way...you have everything except what you want at the moment? But I have no complaints. A little will of the wisp is flying around my awareness, but it will come in for a landing... Providence will see to that. Sooner or later I/ll see it.

Here you go, brisket, salad. Can I get you anything else? Something to drink?

No, no thanks. This is fine.

Yes, yes, this is fine...real fine the way she walks and...and whatever. Oh Red... Who the hell ever said theyd rather be dead than red? What madness. Red is the color of my true loves hair...hmmm the brisket really is pretty good. Salads not bad too. Funny how different dressings taste so different in various places. Same old bowl of shredded lettuce, but sometimes the Italian tastes like Irish sauce. Wonder if they have a particular dressing? Probably mayo and ketchup...with a touch of tabasco. No self-respecting Italian would call this dressing good, but if you forget what its supposed to be and accept it for what it is, a deli dressing, its not so bad. Its like canned spaghetti. Loved it when I was a kid. Nothing like real pasta, but if you forget that its not bad. But of course, you can never really forget whats real and whats a hopeless imitation. Like ol Jimbo. Cant forget he was just imitation people, a piece of detritus that was somehow scraped off the shoes of the fisherman or some ditch digger, and somehow got classified as a human being. World is filled with such insults to the human race. And theyre not all politicians either. Or televangelists. Or even teamsters. Why, some of my best friends are teamsters—wait a minute, lets not go that far. Those bastards... Have to pay more for a loaf of bread and a quart of milk... Oh well, time to take a short walk and get back to work.

Jesus, pictures of the 'Royal Family' on the front page of the paper. What the hell is that all about? If they want to keep those parasites thats fine with me, but why clutter up our papers with stories about bonnie prince charlie and—wait a second...prince...prince... I almost got it. Somethings—of course, Machiavelli. Divide and conquer. Dont let the right hand know what the left is doing. Wait...wait a second...something is happening—ah, the fresh air is good...if you can consider it fresh. So, deception...divide and conquer...well, conquer in a limited sense. Certainly not going to 'take' anything. Royal Family. Why does that keep spinning in my head? Royal Family, Royal Family. What in the hell do they have to do with this? Royal pain in the ass. Who deceives who...whom? Why???? What in the hell can this have to do with Royalty? Royal mess???? Royal screw up???? Royal, Royal... Cincinnati Royals...oh come on. Madness. Well, she is a nutcase...but nothing to do with me. No. Family. What family? Whose family? Family? Family????

Family!!!! Somethings coming together—How in the hell did I get to the park? Oh well, sit on the bench under a tree. Hmmm, surprisingly quiet. Really pleasant. Just a few blocks from the house. Wonder why I never came here before. Nice and quiet too. Damn...birds and everything. Probably a lot of nests. Good trees for them...heavy foliage. Hide from predators. Protect their family. Seems like a lot of energy in nature goes into protecting the family...the klan. Yeah, some wear skirts, some wear sheets. Hey, wait a second. Thats right. Every one wants to protect the family...whatever or whoever you consider your family. From the dumb street kids to the mafia. Its the family. Okay, okay. The family! Must be plenty of them. Special legislation, prosecutors, investigators, undercover agents, witness protection program, an entire legal sub-culture to combat an illegal sub-culture. Yeah, chirp away little birdies...or sing, as they used to say in the old gangster movies. Eddie G and Cagney never sang. They told the bulls where to shove it. Oh, its really starting to come together. Yeah, lets all sing like the birdies sing, tweet tweet... Sammy the Bull. Yeah, thats a good place to start. Probably take a while, but I/ll get all the info I need. I can really feel it happening. Its coming together. Must keep my mind open and just get the information. Leave the results in the hands of Providence. I/ll know what to do when the time is right. I always know... Well, better get back to work—no! Take it easy. Let it continue to gel. Yeah...tomorrows plenty of time. Just let it be...yeah, and present itself to me. Just as it always does.

Is it not joyous to see a man of faith? Indeed, every soul in the Universe rejoices and sings his praises. It takes but one man of faith to transform the world, and thus does my son transform this world of ego and mockery. Oh my faultless son, some day you will hear the Heavens sing, the very stars kneel at your feet. Yet you think not of these things, but only of the task at hand. Meditate well on the task, my son, all has already been given you. Continue to surrender to the task and your awareness will be illuminated at every step. You are the aurora borealis of my life.

Well, what do we have so far...a lot of families loosely connected and/or opposed...a lot of in-laws and out-laws...to coin a phrase. Plenty of rivalry in New York. And elsewhere. Advantage here is I dont want it to look like a normal death...yeah, except that killing each other is a normal death...if they dont kill themselves with cigarettes and espresso. Okay, lets get serious for a minute. The danger is to kill them without getting caught...by them or the police. However, I also have the advantage of not needing to be completely surreptitious. Its important it looks just like any other gangland killing...and god knows there are abundant examples to copy. Safest if done from a distance, but close enough for accuracy. Cant look like an accident. Must make them think another family did it. Havent had a good gang shoot-out for a long time. Before Im through theyll be knocking each other off like a free lunch, free lunch??? Where the hell did that come from? Okay, a jokes a joke, and a good laugh will heal anything, but I have to stay serious long enough to map this out. Now, New York is always the center of attention, so thats where I start. But need to know where else. Must have everything clearly organized and defined before I start. Imperative. Dont need too many cit—yeah...oh yeah, thats right. Important thing is that it looks like somebody is trying to take over the mob...hmmm... Oh shit, wait a minute. Maybe I dont need to concentrate only on the old wise guys. Yeah... Those crazy Russians are driving a lot of people nuts. Hit one...maybe two...wise guy places...yeah, sounds good, one or two of those and then a Russian 'club'. Theyll be at each others throats. Yeah, theyre crazier than the Sicilians. Okay...lets see. I start with a 'social club', maybe even the one Gotti used to go to, and stir up a little trouble. Have to make them believe the Russians are behind it... Whats their favorite thing? Seems like just killing. There must be a method associated with them more than just a few shots in the head???? Yeah, but how would I do—No! Cant take that attitude. Cant start thinking I cant do this or cant do that. Establish the right way to do it and I/ll know how. So... Okay, they love to blow things up, ba boom. But how—relax. Let it come. Well...wiring a car is out. Need to get too close...and its an old wise guy method. Also too neat. Russians are nuts. Theyd blow up a whole building to open a coconut. Want it to look unplanned. Like walking down the street and suddenly deciding to toss a hand-grenade. Real subtle. And obvious. Make it so they figure it has to be the fuckin Russians. Yeah, no kiss of death, no shots in the head and throat, and no last meal. Hey, hold the scungilli, I gotta take care of business here—Right, right. Serious. Okay, so they know its the Russians. The mob is better organized. Should have troops in the streets in minutes...hours. So, I start where???? Hey, I have to drop this for a while. Take a break and get something to eat. No rush. Easy does it. Dont go running around so fast I pass myself. Nice and easy...

...well...I guess thats settled...at least for now. That should make it easy for the wise guys. After all, I do aim to please. Make it as easy as possible to...shall we say...make each others acquaintance. A club in Coney Island is blown up and they visit the Russians in Brighton Beach. Probably take a couple of days. Make sure they know whats happening. Then the Russians will be very perturbed. Who knows what those crazy bastards will do? When the timing is right...Mulberry St. Yeah...sounds good. Then move on. Yeah. Okay. Seems St Louis and New Orleans would be best. Logistics are difficult...yeah...but just seems like theyre the towns. Could lead to such wonderful chaos. Still a lot of work to do. Seems so slow. Month and this is as far as Ive gotten. Oh well, theyre not going anywhere. Best to be thorough. Will have to check those two towns out. Get most of what I need on Internet, but ultimately this is hands-on work. So the plot thickens and the plan hatches... Okay, time to find out how to make an explosive device...nice and small. Yeah... then a delivery system. One that keeps me out of harms way. A light charge. Of course. No need to be too devastating. Risk my neck. Need a substantial explosion, not monumental. Right. Well, that makes it easier. Well, just keep doing the footwork. It will all work out. Never spent so much time on the Net. Knew it was endless, but never checked it out like this. Okay, first things first. Explosives.

...jesus krist, why do I read this shit? Get myself so pissed off...krist, these people are sick...and they make me sick. Got to learn not to read this stuff. Let myself get suckered into a headline and then the next thing I know Im out of my gourd. Screw the ignorant bastards. Okay...enough. Close it out. Whatever. Not going to allow myself to get so pissed off I lose track of my job. Back to the formulas for simple explosives, and not the reasons for blowing up the government... Yeah, that is pretty funny, yours truly the number one defender of the government. Actually nothing incongruous about that. The fact that I accepted the responsibility for freeing us veterans of a viper employed by the government doesnt mean I want to overthrow the government and kill innocent people. Jesus...more than 160 people. Not counting the trauma to the survivors. Kids suddenly without a parent, or parents, parents suddenly without children. My god, innocent little children, babes in arms...theres no words. Look at that, I click off the page and Im sitting here running these things through my head, over and over. Have to stop reaching for incidents to torture myself. Time to get working on this stuff. Should be able to put this all together without too much trouble. Few ingredients. Couple of pieces of wood. What about testing it? Hmmm...good question. Find some desolate area and use a very small amount might not sound any louder than a firecracker. But theres always the possibility it will attract unwanted attention. Unwanted??? any attention is unwanted. I dont know. Where can I go…where???? Plenty of densely wooded areas I can go to. Be unseen. Yeah, but anyone else there will be unseen. And god only knows the consequences. Suppose a fire starts. Last thing I want to do is destroy a woodland. Plus I might be seen. I dont know. Damn. Didnt think this part would be so difficult. Last time I just went ahead and used it and it turned out fine. But this is different…

Or is it? Suppose I just go to the 'club' and hit it. Whatve I lost if it doesnt work? Anything? Well, I might be seen…yeah, possible. But if no damage done what would be the big deal? True, might be a big deal, but seems a lot better, for many reasons, than starting a forest fire. I dont know, feels right to just go to the object of all this. It worked the other times. Yeah, okay, I dont have to decide now. Sleep on it and see what I feel tomorrow. I/ll know. Just like always. Too wound up from reading about those bloodthirsty freaks. Calm down, I/ll know. Okay. Let it go. Tomorrow.

Well…another day another buck and a half. Birds really singing this morning… listen to those finches. Go for it. Remember some little poem about a bird on a window sill singing and bringing up the sun and all that sort of thing and ends with the narrator saying he gently shut the window and crushed his fucking head. I am NOT a morning person. Guess maybe I am. Dont mind the birds singing. Sound good actually. Especially the mockingbirds. Theyll kick in soon. Sort of nice. Why would anyone want to crush a birds head? Theyre really kind of nice. Seems sort of gruesome and messy. Anyway, enough. No doubt theres no need to go testing a device, no matter how small. I/ll just go for it. Putting it together seems simple. Put together the 'delivery device' first...I like that, 'delivery device'. Very official. Type up a little prospectus and submit it to the Defense Department. They may subsidize my endeavor. Shit, go to the CIA and theyll hire me. Yeah, for a while. Until I want to quit. No retirement with those bastards. Nothing like anonymity. Safest way to work. Okay, enough shilly shallying. Time to get to the garage and start making the crossbow.

Okay, lets see if I can hit the target... Whoa, this sucker is tough to load... Well, here goes... Wump, as they say in cartoons. Hmmm, could be worse...a lot worse I guess. Didnt get near where I was aiming...but all I have to do is get it through a doorway or window. Damn, this thing went a couple of inches into this board. Well, a little more practice and I/ll certainly be able to do whats needed. Yeah, better wrap something around the tip to see what that does. Lot of inherent dangers here. Have to wait until I have a clear shot, and certainly cant camp out in front waiting. And driving around with explosives...well, at least its a small amount. This crossbow must be the smallest one in captivity, and collapsible, easy enough to hide...pant leg, sleeve, wherever. Pretty simple and straightforward but still a possibility for problems. Not worried though. Not naive or complacent. Really done the research. Just have a positive sense about the project. Just as I did with the others. Somehow this is more exciting. More danger...from the target and the means.

More cautious. Alter my appearance more. That would be wise. Look as Russian as possible. A lot to practice. Keep it simple. Little make-up. Hat. Coordinate schedule. New York, St Louis, New Orleans. Change of clothes. Appearance. Always aware. Always simple. Digital camera makes it easy. First finish with the 'equipment'. Thank god for technology. Must look crude. Just like them. And senseless. Mr Chameleon. But not totally. Cant really be invisible. But I can look like what Im not. Who was that masked man? Your worst nightmare keemofuckinsabay. Mr Clean is on his way. Clean up the dirt, the scum. Everything sparkling clean. Pick up a few pieces of clothing at Salvation Army. Thrift Shops. A piece here…there. No trail. No links. Just a little ol city boy caught in a redneck world. Exciting. Playing out a fantasy. Cops and robbers. Bang, bang, youre dead. I am not, you missed me. Bull shit! I gotya right between the eyes. No way, you missed by a mile…fuckin redneck.

Damn, this virtual relocation is pretty good. Cant get the specifics I need, but good idea of general layout. Yeah. Good sense of the town. Go through target area. Know all streets…their outlets. Synchronize all actions. Different appearance each time. Inconspicuous. Noticeable last couple of times. Same appearance…clothes. If questioned witnesses have 'general' impression. Looked Russian. Nobody will ever know what a great actor I am. Or planner. Or instigator…*Agent provocateur.* Maybe I should keep a diary? A log book. A record for the future. A memoir of services rendered. Tempting. Very tempting. Too foolish. Insane. Still, when all this is over…satisfying to be the evil genius behind everything. No one will ever know of my genius…as an actor, thinker, planner, as a power for good. Cant let the ego get in the way. Always give it all to Providence. That's enough satisfaction. No manifesto. No diary. No explanation. Take it all to the grave. Oh, this is such a beautiful plan. And the execution will be flawless. Simplicity. Always keep it simple. Small wooden crossbow. Breaks down into a couple of small pieces. Plastique. Extra powdered magnesium for flash.

Ahhh, good to get home. Lot of roaming around. Yeah…very productive. Better log in and let them know Im back.

Lets see how well I remember them. Quick sketch of all of them. Just cov—No. Details. All the details. All pov's. No guess work. Every doorway. Alley. Yeah…that's right, always a trash can here. Light pole away from corner in New Orleans. Little things. Sign in St Louis hides this corner. Little things = big picture…

Yeah, these drawings are just like the ones I made on the spot. Good. Remember all the details. Even graffiti on the dumpster. Very good. Im ready. Primed. Yeah, need to calm down. Easy does it…in and out…in and out… Work for a few days. Routine. Then…a.m. Coney Island, p.m. St Louis; next day, a.m. New Orleans. One, two, three. Boom, boom, boom. Smoke clears, action starts…*re*actions start. Coney Island Im Russian. St Louis, Italian. New Orleans, nondescript…

Yeah, we seen some guy, right, Joey?

Yeah, he was suspicious.

What exactly was he doing?

You know, kinda hanging aroun, suspicious like, right, Joey?

Yeah. Creepy sorta.

Creepy?

Yeah. Musta been a Russian.

Yeah, yeah. He was a Russian.

Back to my basic routine for a few days. Clear my mind. Relax. Must be alert. Each target has a vantage point, couple, where I can be unnoticed with my little bow. Only visible for a second. Then folded and hidden. If Im noticed it will add to deceit. Explosion will tumble images in peoples minds. Whatever they remember out of the ordinary will work to my advantage. Theyll be convinced its who I want them to see. Always massive confusion after an explosion. Keep the explosions down. Dont want too much…might get innocent people. The powdered magnesium will make a big flash, people cant see for a second. Oh well, enough. Time to eat. Then maybe a movie. Change of pace. Relax.

Is it not a thing of beauty to see a man be simple, thorough and straightforward and thus make the Heavens sing? Is it not a thing of beauty to see the man, nay, anyone, so totally focused on the proper completion of his task? Is not the meticulous attention to the finest detail as beautiful as a Renaissance painting…a Bach fugue? And is it not a thing of beauty to see all this combined with a courageous heart? See the ease with which he walks through airports, unrushed yet adhering to his schedule. Oh, such delight do I take in his very movements, his apparent nonchalance, his indifference to his surroundings, yet nothing is allowed to slip past his awareness. Can any father be more proud of his son? I think not, even though you go back to time immemorial there is no son more pleasing to his fathers eyes.

… I cant believe it. Im back. Cant believe it. Less than 48 hrs. Seems like weeks. Intense. Can feel it now. Starting to. Letting it go. Cold beer and a chair. Ahhhh…. Oh that feels good. Hairy moments. Very. But not a hitch. All done. Boom! Boom! Boom! Just like that. One, two three. Oono, dosey, tracy. Yeah… They got the business. Feel like Ive been running for days. She looked right at me. Aiming. Mouth looked like a tunnel. Eyes bugged. Blinking. Disguise threw her. So did the explosion. Knocked me around too. Little miscalculation. Good thing I positioned myself around that corner. BaBoom! Yeah!!!! Bomb throwers must have been stunned. Yeah… Their club house will need repairs. Splintered, as the saying goes. Cant sit. Another beer will help. Get on line and see what theyre saying…see what the TV has to say…

'…and following up on the explosion on Mott Street Wednesday, the authorities announced that a check reveals that it was definitely not a gas leak but an explosive device of some sort that was responsible. The object apparently was the Italian/American Social Club, which sustained enormous damage. Fortunately, none of the surrounding storefronts sustained more than slight damage. The five occupants of the club are still hospitalized. Hospital spokesperson said that Benjamin (Benny One Ball) Lazarno, and Louis (Luke the Spook) Nagarnno are in critical but stable condition—You have something new, Sally.'

'Yes, I do, Steve. Im here, at the site of the explosion, and there are two young boys who say they think they saw the man responsible. Here, tell us what you saw.'

'Well, you know, we saw this guy—'

'A real weirdo.'

'Yeah, with this weird beard, you know?'

'An it wasnt like, you know, one a those Hasidic guys.'

'Right, he wasnt no Jew.'

'No, he was a Russian.'

'Yeah, he was blond and fuzzy like, you know. An he had an accent.'

'Yeah.'

'What did he say?'

'I dont know, it was Russian, you know?'

'So there you have it, Steve, an eye witness account.'

'Thanks, Sally. I presume he didnt mean "Warm and Fuzzy".'

'That was awful, Steve.'

'Sorry about that. In other news—'

Well...can you imagine that? They think it was a Russian. God, how easy to plant a seed and mis-lead. Lets see what we have from points west and south. Well, lets see whats going on in St Louis... Here we go...BLAST KILLS ONE INJURES SIX. Hmmm...explosive device... Social Club...okay, enough of that, what...okay, here we are...the deceased evidently was walking across the room when the blast occurred and must have been immediately on top of the device and taken the major force of the explosion, which literally tore his body into a dozen pieces—oh, thats nice—and so the others received serious, though relatively minor injuries. Well, well, well, talk about freaky events. Hell, hes a hero. Gave his life for his friends. What greater gift could he give than his life for his friends. Thats what I love about these guys, their undying sense of loyalty. All for one and one for all. Here, here. Pip, pip, and all that sort of rot. Rest In Peace brother, for all men are my brothers. Can a sparrow fall from the sky without a tear falling from my eye? Go in peace to your maker you slime-ball. Lets see what else…no, no mention of any other activity, no gang war…yet. Right. Key word: yet. Leave us take a look at our friends, our goombas, in Lousyana. Ah huh, here we go. Another kaboom. Oh, and a fire. An hour to put it out. Hey, 8 hospitalized here, 3 in very critical condition. Not certain they will live through the night. Yeah, why bother? Going to go belly up some day anyway, may just as well do it now. What the hell, youre already in the hospital. Why waste the trip? You went to all the trouble to get yourself blown up you may just as well go to the big Social Club in the sky. But its up to you Sylvester. Hey, if you want to live, more power to you. Wow, pretty good pictures. Must have been someone right there. Really clicked away. Concentrated on the building. Obviously not a pro. No shots of peoples expressions. There should be something in the story about a…up, here it is. A spectator and witness was hospitalized with extreme emotional trauma after informing the authorities that she saw the man responsible for the explosion and said he looked like Groucho Marx and was aiming a space weapon at the building. She said it looked like a ray gun made of some special material she had never seen before, probably from outer space. She continually referred to Grouchos nose and mustache… Ha ha ha, I knew it, I knew it. Nothing more subtle than being overly obvious. A real stroke of genius putting on those Groucho glasses with the nose and mustache. I almost froze when she walked around the corner, a one in a million, while I was aiming my little crossbow, but when she stared I just wrinkled my forehead and those monstrous eyebrows and said, 'Say the magic word,' and let go the bolt with the plastique. Kaboom. One in a million. Wrong place at the wrong time. Hope she recovers. Traumatic running into Groucho with a ray gun, all these years after he died. That will get you to give up drinking, or whatever youre doing. Maybe I should go visit her. Oh god, that would really destroy her…but Im telling you, doctor, Groucho was here yesterday. No, I shouldnt even think of things like that. I dont want her to have any troubles. Dont worry sweetheart, I wont send you any pictures of Groucho. Not even a signed 8x10 glossy. Alright, enough. Time to eat. Nuke some popcorn and open another beer. A night to be savored. Should be some more details tomorrow. Who knows, there might even be some retaliation in the offing. Who knows? The shadow do. Yeah, the shadow do do do. Oh god, how luxurious I feel. How providential, to coin a phrase. No,

I feel festive. Thats what it is, festive. And celebratory. I am truly king of all I survey. Im on top of the world Ma. Yeah, he went kaboom too. But not yours truly. The closest thing to kaboom in my life is the popping of corn. Best thing is an old movie. Or Bugs Bunny or Rocky and Bullwinkle. We/ll see. Starting to feel a little tired now that Im unlaxing. Should have a good, restful sleep tonight. Tomorrow will be another beautiful day, with or without our feathered friends chirping. So, lets see whats happening on the oldies but goodies channel…

…ah yes, chirp, chirp, chirp…chirp away you feathered fiends. You must be what Beethoven heard during his walks through his beloved woods…yeah, until he went deaf. Wonder how long he was able to hear them? He certainly heard them in his head long after the death of his ears. But of course he did not have to worry about them leaving their calling card on a newly washed and waxed car…with the Amorall treatment. Guess there are no cats around, theyre not sounding disturbed. So sing on, but remember I put in a good word for you with the neighborhood cats so leave that blue Lexus alone, okay? Oh, the day feels good. Time to eat. Yeah…breakfast, a walk to that bench, and sit and listen to the birds and read the paper. Yeah, thats a good one, never thought of that, but the newspaper is like an updated carrier pigeon. Communication. Always the most important thing on earth. Rothschilds realized a fortune because they knew of Napoleons defeat before the English government. Drums, smoke, screeching, pigeons, teletype, radio, whatever, we/re no better off than when we were banging a couple of sticks together. We can get information back and forth almost instantly but it doesnt stop the slaughter. So whats the point??? making more money? We have information coming out of our asses and we still cant communicate. Oh well, no longer a concern of mine. I communicate efficiently enough for me. Yeah, it is a shame I cant communicate this to someone, but such is life. At least I know the right people are getting the message. Hey, thats pretty good. Well, time to perambulate, eat, then read. Wonder if the redhead will be working. Seems like months since Ive been there. Cant remember what shift she has. Actually, dont know if they always have the same shift. Probably rotate. Well, anyway, a little food will go just fine. Time to join the birds and start the day with a song, even when things go wrong...

This truly is a delightful spot. No point in weeping about not having found it sooner. Enjoy it today. Far enough away from traffic to hear the breeze in the trees. Hope the birds respect me. Have to come here on a warm night. See the stars peeking between the trees. No. Cant let my mind go wandering like that. Need to stay aware. Must make it habitual...right here right now. Always aware. Like what Im reading in the paper. Millions starving; hundreds of thousands massacred; women and children hacked and burned... Dont even know if this is todays paper, yesterdays, last week, last year...same old same old. What a world. Nothing but violence, mayhem, slaughter, everything but peace. I dont know, mans inhumanity to—Oh no! I dont believe it! What sort of madness is this? How long are they going to allow this sort of thing to continue? Measures should be taken to stop it instantly. Instantly!!!! This is utterly disgraceful. Oh yeah, you bet your sweet patouzy it is. Man oh man…jumpin bald headed codfish. Oh zippidy do dah, zippidy yay, my oh my what a wonderful day… Authorities fear an outbreak of gang warfare in Brooklyn. Yesterday at 9:42 a.m., a bomb ex—yeah, yeah, we know all about that, lets get to the good part wh—here we go, lets see, yeah, A bar, a reputed hangout for the Russian mafia, in Brighton Beach was attacked with grenades and automatic weapon fire—Alright! Right the fuck on!—First reports place the damage to the bar as 'total', and 4 are confirmed dead, 5 more seriously injured. The fire depart—yeah, yeah. Oh god, this is exciting. Careful now, careful. In…out… In…out… Nice and easy. Get too excited the top of my head will blow off. After all the time I spent trying, this is no time to succeed. Have to take it easy. Dont want a heart attack. Oh god, I feel so good it hurts. Feeling dizzy for krists sake. Okay now, just keep breathing in…out…nice and slow…nice and easy. Yeah. Krist, people are predictable. Always jumping to conclusions. All out war. Havent had an all out war in Brooklyn for years. Wonder if they still know how to do it. Do the wise guys today know how to hit the mattresses? Oh how wonderful…how fucking delicious. Theyre killing each other. Can you believe these assholes? I knew theyd do this. I absolutely knew it, yet Im still surprised at how stupid greed can make them.

Well, thank god for that. Wonder if anythings happening elsewhere???? Doesnt seem to be anything in the paper. See whats on the Net later. Im sure theyll follow suit. Wow, my chest is still pounding, but its getting better…hearts slowing down. Better just sit here for a while. Yeah…breeze feels good. I/ll be fine in a few minutes. Dont think Ive ever been hit with so much excitement at once. This is better than all the others. To get them to kill each other is sublime, absolutely sublime. It will be a while before I can walk, I can feel it. Whats the difference. No need to move. Sit as long as I want. Should have brought some nuts for squirrels. Have nothing to do and plenty of time to do it in. Yowza, yowza, yowza… But all that aside Mrs Lincoln, what did you think of the play? Yeah, the play, the plays the thing. What do we play next? Oh, there are so many candidates. A lot of real winners. Bankers, Lawyers, so many deserving of a little 'attention'. Like that Insurance Commissioner Quackenbush. Quackenbush…if you had a name like that youd be a low-life weasel too. Runs to Hawaii and gets away with it. Who, Quackendabush? No Chico, thats a bird in the bush, and it gathers no moss. Man, does he deserve a little 'attention'. But nothing gratuitous. No punishment for the sake of punishing…well, that is the American way, punish, punish and then punish. Dont want to fall into that punishment trap. Good god, thats the last thing I need. Leave that to the christians. Oh well, no point in wasting my time on concentrating on them, more important fish to fry. Hmmm, frying fish, now that sounds like a good idea. If

I knew a little more about electricity I just might be able to pull that off. Krist, the entire insurance industry is filled with deserving individuals. Especially HMOs. Lordy, lordy, lordy, are they ever deshpicable. Yeah, you tellem Daffy. And theres Chain Saw Al. What a dinner guest hed make. 'Tell me, Albert, how many thousand employees did you discharge today?' The problem is once you start thinking of the slime-balls in the world the list is endless. Well, I do have plenty of time…a lifetime actually. Now that I know what my purpose is in life I can relax and be certain I dont dissipate my energies. Take the actions of 'elimination' that are the most efficacious. Everyone needs a purpose for living. Even those vermin like Barnard. But we need a higher purpose… Yeah, nobility. Must be noble in thought and action. Only way to noble results… Yeah…guess that excitement is calming down. Stroll home soon. Might be a good idea to take a trip. Change of scenery. Good for the mind…and soul. Yeah…I like that idea. Bahamas…or Costa Rica. Now that sounds great. Yeah! Costa Rica. Kick back for a few weeks, let these last months go… hmm, year or so actually. What do you know? Yeah, let it drain away. Refresh my body, mind and spirit. Sort of empty myself out so Providence can show me the way to my next venture. Yowza, yowza, yowza…

…damn, I heard that Costa Rica was the ultimate place, but this is beyond… What a spectacular view…trees, underbrush, ocean, sun shimmering and reflecting…and no army. Beyond paradise. Yeah, tomorrow I/ll go to the rainforest. And who knows after that. And theyre still knocking each other off...and its spread to Chicago and Miami. Ohhh, how beautiful...warm sun, cool breeze, cold drink and those stupid *pisanos* and Russians are still knocking each other off. Yes indeed, life is worth living afterall.

Amen

MARION BOYARS PUBLISHERS: selected fiction

THE ROOM

Hubert Selby Jr.

In his remand cell, a small-time petty criminal surrenders himself to the sadistic fantasies of hatred, rage and despair trapped inside him. This terrifying, claustrophobic descent into the isolated mind of a man locked away from society becomes, in Selby's literary tour de force, a bruising vision of a world deprived of love. By giving such a vivid picture of one man's hopelessness, Selby forces us to confront the blame that must be borne by a society capable of allowing such despair to be silently ignored. The blistering follow-up to Selby's best selling cult classic *Last Exit to Brooklyn*, *The Room* still has the power to provoke, to chill and to disturb.

'Selby's place is in the front rank of American novelists ... to understand his work is to understand the anguish of America.' – *New York Times Book Review*

'It is the clash of aspiration, fantasy and desire with the boundaries of the purely contingent that provides the drama of Selby's work and its ferocious poetry.' – *Times Literary Supplement*

'One must be grateful to Selby for his fatal vision and strong, original talent.' – *Newsweek*

'Selby has a classic sense of the absurd, a foolproof ear and a great heart.' – *Terry Southern*

'A major American writer of this century.' – *Los Angeles Times*

REQUIEM FOR A DREAM

Hubert Selby Jr.

Requiem for a Dream, now a major film by cult director Darren Aronofsky, is a modern-day fable set in New York. Lonely widow Sara Goldfarb nurtures fantasies about appearing on prime-time television, while her son Harry, along with his girlfriend Marion and buddy Tyrone C Love, plans his break into big-time drug dealing. Their eyes fixed on an impossible future they move blindly onwards, contorting their lives into coils of self-deception as they struggle to keep their dreams alive.

'Selby's *Requiem for a Dream* clearly marks him as a major American author, of a stature with William S Burroughs and Joseph Heller.'
– *Los Angeles Times*

'An American masterpiece.' – *Los Angeles Times*

UK market only

THE DEMON

Hubert Selby Jr.

Harry White is a man haunted by a satyr's lust and an obsessive need for sin and retribution. The more Harry succeeds, on the fast track to a good marriage and a well-paid corporate job, the more desperate he becomes, as a life of petty crime leads to fraud and murder and, eventually, to apocalyptic violence.

'There is enough of Harry White in our own vagrant daydreams and angry fantasies to attach us to Selby's grim story and to validate his conviction that aberrance is a matter of definition and degree, not of kind. Selby has a brilliant ear ... once again he confirms his amazing power of expressing human darkness.' – *Newsweek*

'Selby, author of *Last Exit to Brooklyn*, has pinned down the captive mind, opened it up and mapped its darkest and most vicious pathways.' – *The Guardian*

'A devastating, dark, perfect novel.' – *Chicago Sun Times*

'He has a deep compassion, a straightforward vision of decency and kindness – important in our drab and shallow age – and is probably one of the six best novelists writing in the English language.' – *Financial Times*

'A major American author, of a stature with William S. Burroughs and Joseph Heller.' – *Los Angeles Times*

THE WILLOW TREE

Hubert Selby Jr.

Bobby is young and black. He shares a cramped apartment in the south Bronx with his mother, his younger brothers and sisters and the ceaselessly scratching rats that infest the wall behind his bed. Barely a teenager, he is old beyond his years. The best thing in Bobby's life is Maria, his Hispanic friend. They are in love and they have big plans for the summer ahead.

Their lives are irrevocably shattered, however, when a vicious street gang attack the couple on their way to school. With Bobby savagely beaten, and Maria lying blind and terrified in hospital, engulfed by the pain of her badly burned face, *The Willow Tree* takes the reader on a volcanically powerful trip through the lives of America's dispossessed inner-city dwellers.

'Like Dante, Selby deploys street slang, common speech, argot and scatology to create high poetic art ... it seems to derive from the greatest American poetry – Whitman, Pound, Williams, Olson...' – *The Nation*

'His work is as affecting as Daumier's great proletarian drawings.' – *Booklist*

'Always and everywhere this calm concern for people – nice people, rough people, failures. It is not only that Mr Selby conveys great compassion. It is also that he shows the essential importance of every human being, whatever the abilities or intellect. All this is projected in writing that is spare and sharp; and completely convincing.' – *Daily Telegraph*

'No serious reader can possibly dismiss Selby. He brings a scorching light to a limited area of human existence, which most people know of, but do not know.' – *Newsweek*

MY MOTHER, MADAME EDWARDA AND THE DEAD MAN

Georges Bataille
Translated by Austryn Wainhouse
With essays by Yukio Mishima and Ken Hollings

These three short pieces of erotic prose fuse elements of sex and spirituality in a highly personal vision of the flesh. They present a world in which the holy horrors of sex and the anguish of heightened awareness struggle against the stultifying spiritual inertia of social order and reason. Each narrative contains a sense of intoxication and insanity so carefully delineated by its author that it infects the reader. 'My Mother' illuminates a young man's incestuous passions following his father's death, while 'Madame Edwarda' and 'The Dead Man' offer disturbing insights into human corruption. This volume also contains Bataille's own introductions to the texts, together with an autobiographical statement and essays by Yukio Mishima and Ken Hollings.

'My Mother is a unique Bildungsroman of a young man's sexual initiation and corruption by his mother.' – *Publishers Weekly*

'Heaves with necrophiliac undercurrents.' – *The Observer*

'Bataille is one of the most important writers of this century. He broke with traditional narrative to tell us what has never been told before.' – *Michel Foucault*

'The power of Bataille's prose is still impressive, his capacity to shock still compelling.' – *Literary Review*

'Bataille's work deals basically with one issue only: the experience of the edge, that is, living at the very limits of life, at the extreme, at the borderline of possibilities.'
– *Bloomsbury Review*

L'ABBE C

Georges Bataille

Translated by Philip A Facey

Told in a series of first-person accounts, *L'Abbe C* is a startling account of the intense and terrifying relationship between twin brothers, Charles and Robert. Charles is a modern libertine dedicated to vice and depravity; Robert is a priest so devout that he is nicknamed 'L'Abbé'. As the story progresses, the suffocating atmosphere of the novel becomes increasingly permeated with illness, breakdown and eventual death. As in *Blue of Noon* and *Story of the Eye*, Bataille has succeeded in portraying the darkest and most profound aspects of human experience with amazing strength and dispassionate objectivity.

'Essentially a psychological novel in which the emotions of the characters determine the movement of the story from beginning to end; explicit sex is absent. The style is crisp and this translation is quite remarkable ... always faithful to the spirit.' – *New York Times Book Review*

'Bataille is now recognised in France as one of the most challenging and original writers of our century. English translations of his work are long overdue, and one can only welcome the opportunity for English-speaking readers to discover this major modern thinker.' – *Leo Bersani*

'Bataille intellectualizes the erotic as he eroticizes the intellect ... reading him can be a disturbing kind of game.' – *New York Times*

PROZAC HIGHWAY

Persimmon Blackbridge

'When your car is spinning out of control heading for the guard rail, you have all the time in the world.'

Losing her nerve and burning out fast, hardcore lesbian performance artist Jam has trouble coping with the outside world. Her best friend and former lover, Roz, thinks Jam's losing it, big time. Her doctor thinks Prozac is the answer. Meanwhile, Jam finds love, comfort and support from ThisIsCrazy, a talk room on the Internet, where she trades messages and shards of hard-bitten wisdom about treatment and withdrawal with the likes of Fruitbat, Junior and D'isMay. Tough, funny and sexy, *Prozac Highway* packs a sweet punch. Think *Tales of the City* in cyberspace and click onto Persimmon Blackbridge's dazzling literary breakthrough.

'Jam and her fellow survivors are smart, funny and excruciatingly self-aware. Highly recommended for all collections.'
– *Library Journal*

'Hilarious.' – *An Advocate Top Ten Selection*

'Cynical wit, sexually explicit imagery and a pinch of pessimism.' – *The Observer*

'Candid, bleakly funny and very, very clever, this is cyber-fiction at its very best.' – Nick Johnstone, *Uncut*

'A beautiful portrait ... Blackbridge writes humorous, intimate, wonderfully restrained prose perfectly attuned to her narrator's vivid inner life ... a tour de force.' – *Publishers Weekly*

LOSING EUGENIO

Geneviève Brisac

Translated from the French by J.A. Underwood

In a small flat in Paris, a single mother, Nouk, lives with her son, Eugenio. As winter sets in, she invents a fairytale Christmas, with wonderful presents and guests. But reality keeps breaking through the brittle façade that Nouk has constructed. This bleakly tender novel tackles the complicated fears and emotions experienced by a lone parent as it offers a wry and honest account of the life of a woman – and a mother – at the edge of her resources. Highly acclaimed winner of the Prix Femina, *Losing Eugenio* has sold over 150,000 copies in France.

'As soon as I finished Geneviève Brisac's *Losing Eugenio*, I started it again. Sometimes a novel is so good, there's no choice.' – *Uncut*

'Marvellous, touching.' – *Time Out*

'Brisac has a light touch.' – *Times Literary Supplement*

'Geneviève Brisac writes like a slipped smile ... and the edge of a soft scalpel.' – *L'Express*

DEAR SHAMELESS DEATH

Latife Tekin
Translated by Saliha Paker & Mel Kenne

A strange, magical story of a young girl growing up in modern Turkey, from her birth in a small rural village haunted by fairies and demons to her traumatic move to the big city. Based on her own childhood, Tekin's literary debut marked a turning point in Turkish fiction. Concentrating on a daughter's struggle against her overbearing mother set against the pressures of a rapidly changing society, *Dear Shameless Death* is a fantastic, hallucinatory novel, which gives an insight into what it means to be a woman growing up in Turkey today.

'I am,' Tekin has written, 'of the generation which found itself in the middle of a political battle the minute I stepped out of childhood.' A major best seller in her native Turkey, Tekin remains politically active and has published a number of literary works. Her second novel, *Berji Kristin: Tales of the Garbage Hills,* is also available from Marion Boyars Publishers.

'I have never read another book like this one. And perhaps you haven't either. True originality is unusually difficult to define because it gives the impression of existing for the first time and this – fortunately – precludes generalisations ... She has written down what before had never been written down. Other books by other writers will follow – perhaps have already followed – but their, and our, debt to her is enormous.' – John Berger

'A nihilistic wit reminiscent of Samuel Beckett.' – *Independent on Sunday*